Favorite Fairy Tales

(Twelve magical fairy tales for all ages)

STUDENTS UNIVERSE
2019

STUDENTS UNIVERSE
(An imprint of Black Eagle Books)

USA address:
7464 Wisdom Lane, Dublin, OH 43016

India address:
E/312, Trident Galaxy, Kalinga Nagar,
Bhubaneswar-751003, Odisha, India

E-mail: info@blackeaglebooks.org
Website: www.blackeaglebooks.org

FAVORITE FAIRY TALES

Copyright © **Students Universe**

Cover & Interior Design: Ezy's Publication

ISBN- 978-1-64560-054-1 (Paperback)

Printed in United States of America

C o n t e n t s

The Ugly Duckling
Hans Christian Andersen

IT was lovely summer weather in the country, and the golden corn, the green oats, and the haystacks piled up in the meadows looked beautiful. The stork walking about on his long red legs chattered in the Egyptian language, which he had learnt from his mother. The corn-fields and meadows were surrounded by large forests, in the midst of which were deep pools. It was, indeed, delightful to walk about in the country. In a sunny spot stood a pleasant old farm-house close by a deep river, and from the house down to the water side grew great burdock leaves, so high, that under the tallest of them a little child could stand upright. The spot was as wild as the center of a thick wood. In this snug retreat sat a duck on her nest, watching for her young brood to hatch; she was beginning to get tired of her task, for the little ones were a long time coming out of their shells, and she seldom had any visitors. The other ducks liked much better to swim about in the river than to climb the slippery banks, and sit under a burdock leaf, to have a gossip with her. At length one shell cracked, and then another, and from each egg came a living creature that lifted its head and cried, "Peep, peep." "Quack, quack," said the mother, and then they all quacked as well as they could, and looked about them on every side at the large green leaves. Their mother allowed them to look as much as they liked, because green is good for the eyes. "How large the world is," said the young ducks, when they found how much more room they now had than while they were inside the egg-shell. "Do you imagine this is the whole world?" asked the mother; "Wait till you have seen the garden; it stretches far beyond that to the parson's field, but I have never ventured to such a distance. Are you all out?" she continued, rising; "No, I declare, the largest egg lies there still. I wonder how long this is to last, I am quite tired of it;" and she seated herself again on the nest.

"Well, how are you getting on?" asked an old duck, who paid her a visit.

"One egg is not hatched yet," said the duck, "it will not break. But just look at all the others, are they not the prettiest little ducklings you ever saw? They are the image of their father, who is so unkind, he never comes to see."

"Let me see the egg that will not break," said the duck; "I have no doubt it is a turkey's egg. I was persuaded to hatch some once, and after all my care and trouble with the young ones, they were afraid of the water. I quacked and clucked, but all to no purpose. I could not get them to venture in. Let me look at the egg. Yes, that is a turkey's egg; take my advice, leave it where it is and teach the other children to swim."

"I think I will sit on it a little while longer," said the duck; "as I have sat so long already, a few days will be nothing."

"Please yourself," said the old duck, and she went away.

At last the large egg broke, and a young one crept forth crying, "Peep, peep." It was very large and ugly. The duck stared at it and exclaimed, "It is very large and not at all like the others. I wonder if it really is a turkey. We shall soon find it out, however when we go to the water. It must go in, if I have to push it myself."

On the next day the weather was delightful, and the sun shone brightly on the green burdock leaves, so the mother duck took her young brood down to the water, and jumped in with a splash. "Quack, quack," cried she, and one after another the little ducklings jumped in. The water closed over their heads, but they came up again in an instant, and swam about quite prettily with their legs paddling under them as easily as possible, and the ugly duckling was also in the water swimming with them.

"Oh," said the mother, "that is not a turkey; how well he uses his legs, and how upright he holds himself! He is my own child, and he is not so very ugly after all if you look at him properly. Quack, quack! come with me now, I will take you into grand society, and introduce you to the farmyard, but you must keep close to me or you may be trodden upon; and, above all, beware of the cat."

When they reached the farmyard, there was a great disturbance, two families were fighting for an eel's head, which, after all, was carried off by the cat. "See, children, that is the way of the world," said the mother duck, whetting her beak, for she would have liked the eel's head herself. "Come, now, use your legs, and let me see how well you can behave. You must bow your heads prettily to that old duck yonder; she is the highest born of them all, and has Spanish blood, therefore, she is well off. Don't you see she has a red flag tied to her leg, which is something very grand, and a great honor for a duck; it shows that everyone is anxious not to lose her, as she can be recognized both by man and beast. Come, now, don't turn your toes, a well-bred duckling spreads his feet wide apart, just like his father and mother, in this way; now bend your neck, and say 'quack.'"

The ducklings did as they were bid, but the other duck stared, and said, "Look, here comes another brood, as if there were not enough of us already! and what a queer looking object one of them is; we don't want him here," and then one flew out and bit him in the neck.

"Let him alone," said the mother; "he is not doing any harm."

"Yes, but he is so big and ugly," said the spiteful duck "and therefore he must be turned out."

"The others are very pretty children," said the old duck, with the rag on her leg, "all but that one; I wish his mother could improve him a little."

"That is impossible, your grace," replied the mother; "he is not pretty; but he has a very good disposition, and swims as well or even better than the others. I think he will grow up pretty, and perhaps be smaller; he has remained too long in the egg, and therefore his figure is not properly formed;" and then she stroked his neck and smoothed the feathers, saying, "It is a drake, and therefore not of so much consequence. I think he will grow up strong, and able to take care of himself."

"The other ducklings are graceful enough," said the old duck. "Now make yourself at home, and if you can find an eel's head, you can bring it to me."

And so they made themselves comfortable; but the poor duckling, who had crept out of his shell last of all, and looked so ugly, was bitten and pushed and made fun of, not only by the ducks, but by all the poultry. "He is too big," they all said, and the turkey cock, who had been born into the world with spurs, and fancied himself really an emperor, puffed himself out like a vessel in full sail, and flew at the duckling, and became quite red in the head with passion, so that the poor little thing did not know where to go, and was quite miserable because he was so ugly and laughed at by the whole farmyard. So it went on from day to day till it got worse and worse. The poor duckling was driven about by everyone; even his brothers and sisters were unkind to him, and would say, "Ah, you ugly creature, I wish the cat would get you," and his mother said she wished he had never been born. The ducks pecked him, the chickens beat him, and the girl who fed the poultry kicked him with her feet. So at last he ran away, frightening the little birds in the hedge as he flew over the palings.

"They are afraid of me because I am ugly," he said. So he closed his eyes, and flew still farther, until he came out on a large moor, inhabited by wild ducks. Here he remained the whole night, feeling very tired and sorrowful.

In the morning, when the wild ducks rose in the air, they stared at their new comrade. "What sort of a duck are you?" they all said, coming around him.

He bowed to them, and was as polite as he could be, but he did not reply to their question. "You are exceedingly ugly," said the wild ducks, "but that will not matter if you do not want to marry one of our family."

Poor thing! he had no thoughts of marriage; all he wanted was permission to lie among the rushes, and drink some of the water on the moor. After he had been on the moor two days, there came two wild geese, or rather goslings, for they had not been out of the egg long, and were very saucy. "Listen, friend," said one of them to the duckling, "you are so ugly, that we like you very well. Will you go with us, and become a bird of passage? Not far from here is another moor, in which there are some pretty wild geese, all unmarried. It is a chance for you to get a wife; you may be lucky, ugly as you are."

"Pop, pop," sounded in the air, and the two wild geese fell dead among the rushes, and the water was tinged with blood. "Pop, pop," echoed far and wide in the distance, and whole flocks of wild geese rose up from the rushes. The sound continued from every direction, for the sportsmen surrounded the moor, and some were even seated on branches of trees, overlooking the rushes. The blue smoke from the guns rose like clouds over the dark trees, and as it floated away across the water, a number of sporting dogs bounded in among the rushes, which bent beneath them wherever they went. How they terrified the poor duckling! He turned away his head to hide it under his wing, and at the same moment a large terrible dog passed quite near him. His jaws were open, his tongue hung from his mouth, and his eyes glared fearfully. He thrust his nose close to the duckling, showing his sharp teeth, and then, "splash, splash," he went into the water without touching him, "Oh," sighed the duckling, "how thankful I am for being so ugly; even a dog will not bite me." And so he lay quite still, while the shot rattled through the rushes, and gun after gun was fired over him. It was late in the day before all became quiet, but even then the poor young thing did not dare to move. He waited quietly for several hours, and then, after looking carefully around him, hastened away from the moor as fast as he could. He ran over field and meadow till a storm arose, and he could hardly struggle against it. Towards evening, he reached a poor little cottage that seemed ready to fall, and only remained standing because it could not decide on which side to fall first. The storm continued so violent, that the duckling could go no farther; he sat down by the cottage, and then he noticed that the door was not quite closed in consequence of one of the hinges having given way. There was therefore a narrow opening near the bottom large enough for him to slip through, which he did very quietly, and got a shelter for the night. A woman, a tom cat, and a hen lived in this cottage. The tom cat, whom the mistress called, "My little son," was a great favorite; he could raise his back, and purr, and could even throw out sparks from his fur if it were stroked the wrong way. The hen had very short legs, so she was called "Chickie short legs." She laid good eggs, and her mistress loved her as if she had been her own child. In the morning, the strange visitor was discovered, and the tom cat began to purr, and the hen to cluck.

"What is that noise about?" said the old woman, looking round the room, but her sight was not very good; therefore, when she saw the duckling she thought it must be a fat duck, that had strayed from home. "Oh what a prize!" she exclaimed, "I hope it is not a drake, for then I shall have some duck's eggs. I must wait and see." So the duckling was allowed to remain on trial for three weeks, but there were no eggs. Now the tom cat was the master of the house, and the hen was mistress, and they always said, "We and the world," for they believed themselves to be half the world, and the better half too. The duckling thought that others might hold a different opinion on the subject, but the hen would not listen to such doubts. "Can you lay eggs?" she asked. "No." "Then have the goodness to hold your tongue." "Can you raise your back, or purr, or throw out sparks?" said the tom cat. "No." "Then you have no right to express an opinion when sensible people are speaking." So the duckling sat in a corner, feeling very low spirited, till the sunshine and the fresh air came into the room through the open door, and then he began to feel such a great longing for a swim on the water, that he could not help telling the hen.

"What an absurd idea," said the hen. "You have nothing else to do, therefore you have foolish fancies. If you could purr or lay eggs, they would pass away."

"But it is so delightful to swim about on the water," said the duckling, "and so refreshing to feel it close over your head, while you dive down to the bottom."

"Delightful, indeed!" said the hen, "why you must be crazy! Ask the cat, he is the cleverest animal I know, ask him how he would like to swim about on the water, or to dive under it, for I will not speak of my own opinion; ask our mistress, the old woman- there is no one in the world more clever than she is. Do you think she would like to swim, or to let the water close over her head?"

"You don't understand me," said the duckling.

"We don't understand you? Who can understand you, I wonder? Do you consider yourself more clever than the cat, or the old woman? I will say nothing of myself. Don't imagine such nonsense, child, and thank your good fortune that you have been received here. Are you not in a warm room, and in society from which you may learn something. But you are a chatterer, and your company is not very agreeable. Believe me, I speak only for your own good. I may tell you unpleasant truths, but that is a proof of my friendship. I advise you, therefore, to lay eggs, and learn to purr as quickly as possible."

"I believe I must go out into the world again," said the duckling.

"Yes, do," said the hen. So the duckling left the cottage, and soon found water on which it could swim and dive, but was avoided by all other animals, because of its ugly appearance. Autumn came, and the leaves in the forest turned to orange and gold. then, as winter approached, the wind caught them as they fell and whirled them in the cold air. The clouds, heavy with hail and snow-flakes, hung low in the sky, and the raven stood on the ferns crying, "Croak, croak." It made one shiver with cold to look at him. All this was very sad for the poor little duckling. One evening, just as the sun set amid radiant clouds, there came a large flock of beautiful birds out of the bushes. The duckling had never seen any like them before. They were swans, and they curved their graceful necks, while their soft plumage shown with dazzling whiteness. They uttered a singular cry, as they spread their glorious wings and flew away from those cold regions to warmer countries across the sea. As they mounted higher and higher in the air, the ugly little duckling felt quite a strange sensation as he watched them. He whirled himself in the water like a wheel, stretched out his neck towards them, and uttered a cry so strange that it frightened himself. Could he ever forget those beautiful, happy birds; and when at last they were out of his sight, he dived under the water, and rose again almost beside himself with excitement. He knew not the names of these birds, nor where they had flown, but he felt towards them as he had never felt for any other bird in the world. He was not envious of these beautiful creatures, but wished to be as lovely as they. Poor ugly creature, how gladly he would have lived even with the ducks had they only given him encouragement. The winter grew colder and colder; he was obliged to swim about on the water to keep it from freezing, but every night the space on which he swam became smaller and smaller. At length it froze so hard that the ice in the water crackled as he moved, and the duckling had to paddle with his legs as well as he could, to keep the space from closing up. He became exhausted at last, and lay still and helpless, frozen fast in the ice.

Early in the morning, a peasant, who was passing by, saw what had happened. He broke the ice in pieces with his wooden shoe, and carried the duckling home to his wife. The warmth revived the poor little creature; but when the children wanted to play with him, the duckling thought they would do him some harm; so he started up in terror, fluttered into the milk-pan, and splashed the milk about the room. Then the woman clapped her hands, which frightened him still more. He flew first into the butter-cask, then into the meal-tub, and out again. What a condition he was in! The woman screamed, and struck at him with the tongs; the children laughed and screamed, and tumbled over each other, in their efforts to catch him; but luckily he escaped. The door stood open; the poor creature could just manage to slip out among the bushes, and lie down quite exhausted in the newly fallen snow.

It would be very sad, were I to relate all the misery and privations which the poor little duckling endured during the hard winter; but when it had passed, he found himself lying one morning in a moor, amongst the rushes. He felt the warm sun shining, and heard the lark singing, and saw that all around was beautiful spring. Then the young bird felt that his wings were strong, as he flapped them against his sides, and rose high into the air. They bore him onwards, until he found himself in a large garden, before he well knew how it had happened. The apple-trees were in full blossom, and the fragrant elders bent their long green branches down to the stream which wound round a smooth lawn. Everything looked beautiful, in the freshness of early spring. From a thicket close by came three beautiful white swans, rustling their feathers, and swimming lightly over the smooth water. The duckling remembered the lovely birds, and felt more strangely unhappy than ever.

"I will fly to those royal birds," he exclaimed, "and they will kill me, because I am so ugly, and dare to approach them; but it does not matter: better be killed by them than pecked by the ducks, beaten by the hens, pushed about by the maiden who feeds the poultry, or starved with hunger in the winter."

Then he flew to the water, and swam towards the beautiful swans. The moment they espied the stranger, they rushed to meet him with outstretched wings.

"Kill me," said the poor bird; and he bent his head down to the surface of the water, and awaited death.

But what did he see in the clear stream below? His own image; no longer a dark, gray bird, ugly and disagreeable to look at, but a graceful and beautiful swan. To be born in a duck's nest, in a farmyard, is of no consequence to a bird, if it is hatched from a swan's egg. He now felt glad at having suffered sorrow and trouble, because it enabled him to enjoy so much better all the pleasure and happiness around him; for the great swans swam round the new-comer, and stroked his neck with their beaks, as a welcome.

Into the garden presently came some little children, and threw bread and cake into the water.

"See," cried the youngest, "there is a new one;" and the rest were delighted, and ran to their father and mother, dancing and clapping their hands, and shouting joyously, "There is another swan come; a new one has arrived."

Then they threw more bread and cake into the water, and said, "The new one is the most beautiful of all; he is so young and pretty." And the old swans bowed their heads before him.

Then he felt quite ashamed, and hid his head under his wing; for he did not know what to do, he was so happy, and yet not at all proud. He had been persecuted and despised for his ugliness, and now he heard them say he was the most beautiful of all the birds. Even the elder-tree bent down its bows into the water before him, and the sun shone warm and bright. Then he rustled his feathers, curved his slender neck, and cried joyfully, from the depths of his heart, "I never dreamed of such happiness as this, while I was an ugly duckling."

Hansel and Gretel
The Brothers Grimm

Hard by a great forest dwelt a poor wood-cutter with his wife and his two children. The boy was called Hansel and the girl Gretel. He had little to bite and to break, and once when great scarcity fell on the land, he could no longer procure daily bread. Now when he thought over this by night in his bed, and tossed about in his anxiety, he groaned and said to his wife, "What is to become of us? How are we to feed our poor children, when we no longer have anything even for ourselves?" "I'll tell you what, husband," answered the woman, "Early to-morrow morning we will take the children out into the forest to where it is the thickest, there we will light a fire for them, and give each of them one piece of bread more, and then we will go to our work and leave them alone. They will not find the way home again, and we shall be rid of them." "No, wife," said the man, "I will not do that; how can I bear to leave my children alone in the forest?—-the wild animals would soon come and tear them to pieces." "O, thou fool!" said she, "Then we must all four die of hunger, thou mayest as well plane the planks for our coffins," and she left him no peace until he consented. "But I feel very sorry for the poor children, all the same," said the man.

The two children had also not been able to sleep for hunger, and had heard what their step-mother had said to their father. Gretel wept bitter tears, and said to Hansel, "Now all is over with us." "Be quiet, Gretel," said Hansel, "do not distress thyself, I will soon find a way to help us." And when the old folks had fallen asleep, he got up, put on his little coat, opened the door below, and crept outside. The moon shone brightly, and the white pebbles which lay in front of the house glittered like real silver pennies. Hansel stooped and put as many of them in the little pocket of his coat as he could possibly get in. Then he went back and said to Gretel, "Be comforted, dear little sister, and sleep in peace, God will not forsake us," and he lay down again in his bed. When day dawned, but before the sun had risen, the woman came and awoke the two children, saying "Get up, you sluggards! we are going into the forest to fetch wood." She gave each a little piece of bread, and said, "There is something for your dinner, but do not eat it up before then, for you will get nothing else." Gretel took the bread under her apron, as Hansel had the stones in his pocket. Then they all set out together on the way to the forest. When they had walked a short time, Hansel stood still and peeped back at the house, and did so again and again. His father said, "Hansel, what art thou looking at there and staying behind for? Mind what thou art about, and do not forget how to use thy legs." "Ah, father," said Hansel, "I am looking at my little white cat, which is sitting up on the roof, and wants to say good-bye to me." The wife said, "Fool, that is not thy little cat, that is the morning sun which is shining on the chimneys." Hansel, however, had not been looking back at the cat, but had been constantly throwing one of the white pebble-stones out of his pocket on the road.

When they had reached the middle of the forest, the father said, "Now, children, pile up some wood, and I will light a fire that you may not be cold." Hansel and Gretel gathered brushwood together, as high as a little hill. The brushwood was lighted, and when the flames were burning very high, the woman said, "Now, children, lay yourselves down by the fire and rest, we will go into the forest and cut some wood. When we have done, we will come back and fetch you away."

Hansel and Gretel sat by the fire, and when noon came, each ate a little piece of bread, and as they heard the strokes of the wood-axe they believed that their father was near. It was not, however, the axe, it was a branch which he had fastened to a withered tree which the wind was blowing backwards and forwards. And as they had been sitting such a long time, their eyes shut with fatigue, and they fell fast asleep. When at last they awoke, it was already dark night. Gretel began to cry and said, "How are we to get out of the forest now?" But Hansel comforted her and said, "Just wait a little, until the moon has risen, and then we will soon find the way." And when the full moon had risen, Hansel took his little sister by the hand, and followed the pebbles which shone like newly-coined silver pieces, and showed them the way.

They walked the whole night long, and by break of day came once more to their father's house. They knocked at the door, and when the woman opened it and saw that it was Hansel and Gretel, she said, "You naughty children, why have you slept so long in the forest?—-we thought you were never coming back at all!" The father, however, rejoiced, for it had cut him to the heart to leave them behind alone.

Not long afterwards, there was once more great scarcity in all parts, and the children heard their mother saying at night to their father, "Everything is eaten again, we have one half loaf left, and after that there is an end. The children must go, we will take them farther into the wood, so that they will not find their way out again; there is no other means of saving ourselves!" The man's heart was heavy, and he thought "it would be better for thee to share the last mouthful with thy children." The woman, however, would listen to nothing that he had to say, but scolded and reproached him. He who says A must say B, likewise, and as he had yielded the first time, he had to do so a second time also.

The children were, however, still awake and had heard the conversation. When the old folks were asleep, Hansel again got up, and wanted to go out and pick up pebbles as he had done before, but the woman had locked the door, and Hansel could not get out. Nevertheless he comforted his little sister, and said, "Do not cry, Gretel, go to sleep quietly, the good God will help us."

Early in the morning came the woman, and took the children out of their beds. Their bit of bread was given to them, but it was still smaller than the time before. On the way into the forest Hansel crumbled his in his pocket, and often stood still and threw a morsel on the ground. "Hansel, why dost thou stop and look round?" said the father, "go on." "I am looking back at my little pigeon which is sitting on the roof, and wants to say good-bye to me," answered Hansel. "Simpleton!" said the woman, "that is not thy little pigeon, that is the morning sun that is shining on the chimney." Hansel, however, little by little, threw all the crumbs on the path.

The woman led the children still deeper into the forest,

where they had never in their lives been before. Then a great fire was again made, and the mother said, "Just sit there, you children, and when you are tired you may sleep a little; we are going into the forest to cut wood, and in the evening when we are done, we will come and fetch you away." When it was noon, Gretel shared her piece of bread with Hansel, who had scattered his by the way. Then they fell asleep and evening came and went, but no one came to the poor children. They did not awake until it was dark night, and Hansel comforted his little sister and said, "Just wait, Gretel, until the moon rises, and then we shall see the crumbs of bread which I have strewn about, they will show us our way home again." When the moon came they set out, but they found no crumbs, for the many thousands of birds which fly about in the woods and fields had picked them all up. Hansel said to Gretel, "We shall soon find the way," but they did not find it. They walked the whole night and all the next day too from morning till evening, but they did not get out of the forest, and were very hungry, for they had nothing to eat but two or three berries, which grew on the ground. And as they were so weary that their legs would carry them no longer, they lay down beneath a tree and fell asleep.

It was now three mornings since they had left their father's house. They began to walk again, but they always got deeper into the forest, and if help did not come soon, they must die of hunger and weariness. When it was mid-day, they saw a beautiful snow-white bird sitting on a bough, which sang so delightfully that they stood still and listened to it. And when it had finished its song, it spread its wings and flew away before them, and they followed it until they reached a little house, on the roof of which it alighted; and when they came quite up to little house they saw that it was built of bread and covered with cakes, but that the windows were of clear sugar. "We will set to work on that," said Hansel, "and have a good meal. I will eat a bit of the roof, and thou, Gretel, canst eat some of the window, it will taste sweet." Hansel reached up above, and broke off a little of the roof to try how it tasted, and Gretel leant against the window and nibbled at the panes. Then a soft voice cried from the room,

"Nibble, nibble, gnaw,
Who is nibbling at my little house?"
The children answered,
"The wind, the wind,
The heaven-born wind,"

and went on eating without disturbing themselves. Hansel, who thought the roof tasted very nice, tore down a great piece of it, and Gretel pushed out the whole of one round window-pane, sat down, and enjoyed herself with it. Suddenly the door opened, and a very, very old woman, who supported herself on crutches, came creeping out. Hansel and Gretel were so terribly frightened that they let fall what they had in their hands. The old woman, however, nodded her head, and said, "Oh, you dear children, who has brought you here? Do come in, and stay with me. No harm shall happen to you." She took them both by the hand, and led them into her little house. Then good food was set before them, milk and pancakes, with sugar, apples, and nuts. Afterwards two pretty little beds were covered with clean white linen, and Hansel and Gretel lay down in them, and thought they were in heaven.

The old woman had only pretended to be so kind; she was in reality a wicked witch, who lay in wait for children, and had only built the little house of bread in order to entice them there. When a child fell into her power, she killed it, cooked and ate it, and that was a feast day with her. Witches have red eyes, and cannot see far, but they have a keen scent like the beasts, and are aware when human beings draw near. When Hansel and Gretel came into her neighborhood, she laughed maliciously, and said mockingly, "I have them, they shall not escape me again!" Early in the morning before the children were awake, she was already up, and when she saw both of them sleeping and looking so pretty, with their plump red cheeks, she muttered to herself, "That will be a dainty mouthful!" Then she seized Hansel with her shriveled hand, carried him into a little stable, and shut him in with a grated door. He might scream as he liked, that was of no use. Then she went to Gretel, shook her till she awoke, and cried, "Get up, lazy thing, fetch some water, and cook something good for thy brother, he is in the stable outside, and is to be made fat. When he is fat, I will eat him." Gretel began to weep bitterly, but it was all in vain, she was forced to do what the wicked witch ordered her.

And now the best food was cooked for poor Hansel, but Gretel got nothing but crab-shells. Every morning the woman crept to the little stable, and cried, "Hansel, stretch out thy finger that I may feel if thou wilt soon be fat." Hansel, however, stretched out a little bone to her, and the old woman, who had dim eyes, could not see it, and thought it was Hansel's finger, and was astonished that there was no way of fattening him. When four weeks had gone by, and Hansel still continued thin, she was seized with impatience and would not wait any longer. "Hola, Gretel," she cried to the girl, "be active, and bring some water. Let Hansel be fat or lean, to-morrow I will kill him, and cook him." Ah, how the poor little sister did lament when she had to fetch the water, and how her tears did flow down over her cheeks!

"Dear God, do help us," she cried. "If the wild beasts in the forest had but devoured us, we should at any rate have died together." "Just keep thy noise to thyself," said the old woman, "all that won't help thee at all."

Early in the morning, Gretel had to go out and hang up the cauldron with the water, and light the fire. "We will bake first," said the old woman, "I have already heated the oven, and kneaded the dough." She pushed poor Gretel out to the oven, from which flames of fire were already darting. "Creep in," said the witch, "and see if it is properly heated, so that we can shut the bread in." And when once Gretel was inside, she intended to shut the oven and let her bake in it, and then she would eat her, too. But Gretel saw what she had in her mind, and said, "I do not know how I am to do it; how do you get in?" "Silly goose," said the old woman, "The door is big enough; just look, I can get in myself!" and she crept up and thrust her head into the oven. Then Gretel gave her a push that drove her far into it, and shut the iron door, and fastened the bolt. Oh! then she began to howl quite horribly, but Gretel ran away, and the godless witch was miserably burnt to death.

Gretel, however, ran like lightning to Hansel, opened his little stable, and cried, "Hansel, we are saved! The old witch is dead!" Then Hansel sprang out like a bird from its cage when the door is opened for it. How they did rejoice and embrace each other, and dance about and kiss each other! And as they had no longer any need to fear her, they went into the witch's house, and in every corner there stood chests full of pearls and jewels. "These are far better than pebbles!" said Hansel, and thrust into his pockets whatever could be got in, and Gretel said, "I, too, will take something home with me," and filled her pinafore full. "But now we will go away." said Hansel, "that we may get out of the witch's forest."

When they had walked for two hours, they came to a great piece of water. "We cannot get over," said Hansel, "I see no foot-plank, and no bridge." "And no boat crosses either," answered Gretel, "but a white duck is swimming there; if I ask her, she will help us over." Then she cried,

"Little duck, little duck, dost thou see,
Hansel and Gretel are waiting for thee?
There's never a plank, or bridge in sight,
Take us across on thy back so white."

The duck came to them, and Hansel seated himself on its back, and told his sister to sit by him. "No," replied Gretel, "that will be too heavy for the little duck; she shall take us across, one after the other." The good little duck did so, and when they were once safely across and had walked for a short time, the forest seemed to be more and more familiar to them, and at length they saw from afar their father's house. Then they began to run, rushed into the parlor, and threw themselves into their father's arms. The man had not known one happy hour since he had left the children in the forest; the woman, however, was dead. Gretel emptied her pinafore until pearls and precious stones ran about the room, and Hansel threw one handful after another out of his pocket to add to them. Then all anxiety was at an end, and they lived together in perfect happiness. My tale is done, there runs a mouse, whosoever catches it, may make himself a big fur cap out of it.

The Selfish Giant
Oscar Wilde

Every afternoon, as they were coming from school, the children used to go and play in the Giant's garden.

It was a large lovely garden, with soft green grass. Here and there over the grass stood beautiful flowers like stars, and there were twelve peach-trees that in the spring-time broke out into delicate blossoms of pink and pearl, and in the autumn bore rich fruit. The birds sat on the trees and sang so sweetly that the children used to stop their games in order to listen to them. "How happy we are here!" they cried to each other.

One day the Giant came back. He had been to visit his friend the Cornish ogre, and had stayed with him for seven years. After the seven years were over he had said all that he had to say, for his conversation was limited, and he determined to return to his own castle. When he arrived he saw the children playing in the garden.

"What are you doing here?" he cried in a very gruff voice, and the children ran away.

"My own garden is my own garden," said the Giant;

"anyone can understand that, and I will allow nobody to play in it but myself." So he built a high wall all round it, and put up a notice-board.

TRESPASSERS
WILL BE
PROSECUTED

He was a very selfish Giant.

The poor children had now nowhere to play. They tried to play on the road, but the road was very dusty and full of hard stones, and they did not like it. They used to wander round the high wall when their lessons were over, and talk about the beautiful garden inside. "How happy we were there," they said to each other.

Then the Spring came, and all over the country there were little blossoms and little birds. Only in the garden of the Selfish Giant it was still winter. The birds did not care to sing in it as there were no children, and the trees forgot to blossom. Once a beautiful flower put its head out from the grass, but when it saw the notice-board it was so sorry for the children that it slipped back into the ground again, and went off to sleep. The only people who were pleased were the Snow and the Frost. "Spring has forgotten this garden," they cried, "so we will live here all the year round." The Snow covered up the grass with her great white cloak, and the Frost painted all the trees silver. Then they invited the North Wind to stay with them, and he came. He was wrapped in furs, and he roared all day about the garden, and blew the chimney-pots down. "This is a delightful spot," he said, "we must ask the Hail on a visit." So the Hail came. Every day for three hours he rattled on the roof of the castle till he broke most of the slates, and then he ran around and round the garden as fast as he could go. He was dressed in grey, and his breath was like ice.

"I cannot understand why the Spring is so late in coming," said the Selfish Giant, as he sat at the window and looked out at his cold white garden; "I hope there will be a change in the weather."

But the Spring never came, nor the Summer. The Autumn gave golden fruit to every garden, but to the Giant's garden she gave none. "He is too selfish," she said. So it was always Winter there, and the North Wind, and the Hail, and the Frost, and the Snow danced about through the trees.

One morning the Giant was lying awake in bed when he heard some lovely music. It sounded so sweet to his ears that he thought it must be the King's musicians passing by. It was really only a little linnet singing outside his window, but it was so long since he had heard a bird sing in his garden that it seemed to him to be the most beautiful music in the world. Then the Hail stopped dancing over his head, and the North Wind ceased roaring, and a delicious perfume came to him through the open casement. "I believe the Spring has come at last," said the Giant; and he jumped out of bed and looked out.

What did he see?

He saw a most wonderful sight. Through a little hole in the wall the children had crept in, and they were sitting in the branches of the trees. In every tree that he could see there was a little child. And the trees were so glad to have the children back again that they had covered themselves with blossoms, and were waving their arms gently above the children's heads. The birds were flying about and twittering with delight, and the flowers were looking up through the green grass and laughing. It was a lovely scene, only in one corner it was still winter. It was the farthest corner of the garden, and in it was standing a little boy. He was so small that he could not reach up to the branches of the tree, and he was wandering all round it, crying bitterly. The poor tree was still quite covered with frost and snow, and the North Wind was blowing and roaring above it. "Climb up! little boy," said the Tree, and it bent its branches down as low as it could; but the boy was too tiny.

And the Giant's heart melted as he looked out. "How selfish I have been!" he said; "now I know why the Spring would not come here. I will put that poor little boy on the top of the tree, and then I will knock down the wall, and my garden shall be the children's playground for ever and ever." He was really very sorry for what he had done.

So he crept downstairs and opened the front door quite softly, and went out into the garden. But when the children saw him they were so frightened that they all ran away, and the garden became winter again. Only the little boy did not run, for his eyes were so full of tears that he did not see the Giant coming. And the Giant stole up behind him and took him gently in his hand, and put him up into the tree. And the tree broke at once into blossom, and the birds came and sang on it, and the little boy stretched out his two arms and flung them round the Giant's neck, and kissed him. And the other children, when they saw that the Giant was not wicked any longer, came running back, and with them came the Spring. "It is your garden now, little children," said the Giant, and he took a great axe and knocked down the wall. And when the people were going to market at twelve o'clock they found the Giant playing with the children in the most beautiful garden they had ever seen.

All day long they played, and in the evening they came to the Giant to bid him good-bye.

"But where is your little companion?" he said: "the

boy I put into the tree." The Giant loved him the best because he had kissed him.

"We don't know," answered the children; "he has gone away."

"You must tell him to be sure and come here to-morrow," said the Giant. But the children said that they did not know where he lived, and had never seen him before; and the Giant felt very sad.

Every afternoon, when school was over, the children came and played with the Giant. But the little boy whom the Giant loved was never seen again. The Giant was very kind to all the children, yet he longed for his first little friend, and often spoke of him. "How I would like to see him!" he used to say.

Years went over, and the Giant grew very old and feeble. He could not play about any more, so he sat in a huge armchair, and watched the children at their games, and admired his garden. "I have many beautiful flowers," he said; "but the children are the most beautiful flowers of all."

One winter morning he looked out of his window as he was dressing. He did not hate the Winter now, for he knew that it was merely the Spring asleep, and that the flowers were resting.

Suddenly he rubbed his eyes in wonder, and looked and looked. It certainly was a marvelous sight. In the farthest corner of the garden was a tree quite covered with lovely white blossoms. Its branches were all golden, and silver fruit hung down from them, and underneath it stood the little boy he had loved.

Downstairs ran the Giant in great joy, and out into the garden. He hastened across the grass, and came near to the child. And when he came quite close his face grew red with anger, and he said, "Who hath dared to wound thee?" For on the palms of the child's hands were the prints of two nails, and the prints of two nails were on the little feet.

"Who hath dared to wound thee?" cried the Giant; "tell me, that I may take my big sword and slay him."

"Nay!" answered the child; "but these are the wounds of Love."

"Who art thou?" said the Giant, and a strange awe fell on him, and he knelt before the little child.

And the child smiled on the Giant, and said to him, "You let me play once in your garden, to-day you shall come with me to my garden, which is Paradise."

And when the children ran in that afternoon, they found the Giant lying dead under the tree, all covered with white blossoms.

The Little Old Woman Who Lived in a Shoe

Joseph Martin Kronheim

Once on a time there was a Little Old Woman who lived in a Shoe. This shoe stood near a great forest, and was so large that it served as a house for the Old Lady and all her children, of which she had so many that she did not know what to do with them.

But the Little Old Woman was very fond of her children, and they only thought of the best way to please her. Strong-arm, the eldest, cut down trees for firewood. Peter made baskets of wicker-work. Mark was chief gardener. Lizzie milked the cow, and Jenny taught the younger children to read.

Now this Little Old Woman had not always lived in a Shoe. She and her family had once dwelt in a nice house covered with ivy, and her husband was a wood-cutter, like Strong-arm. But there lived in a huge castle beyond the forest, a fierce giant, who one day came and laid their house in ruins with his club; after which he carried off the poor wood-cutter to his castle beyond the forest. When the Little Old Woman came home, her house was in ruins and her husband was nowhere to be seen.

Night came on, and as the father did not return, the Old Lady and her family went to search for him. When they came to that part of the wood where the Giant had met their father, they saw an immense shoe. They spent a long time weeping and calling out for their father, but met with no reply. Then the Old Lady thought that they had better take shelter in the shoe until they could build a new house. So Peter and Strong-arm put a roof to it, and cut a door, and turned it into a dwelling. Here they all lived happily for many years, but the Little Old Lady never forgot her husband and his sad fate. Strong-arm, who saw how wretched his mother often was about it, proposed to the next eleven brothers that they should go with him and set their father free from the Giant. Their mother knew the Giant's strength, and would not hear of the attempt, as she feared they would be killed. But Strong-arm was not afraid. He bought a dozen sharp swords, and Peter made as many strong shields and helmets, as well as cross-bows and iron-headed arrows. They were now quite ready; Strong-arm gave the order to march, and they started for the forest. The next day they came in sight of the Giant's Castle. Strong-arm, leaving his brothers in a wood close by, strode boldly up to the entrance, and seized the knocker. The door was opened by a funny little boy with a large head, who kept grinning and laughing.

Strong-arm then walked boldly across the court-yard, and presently met a page, who took off his hat and asked him what he wanted. Strong-arm said he had come to liberate his father, who was kept a prisoner by the Giant; on this the little man said he was sorry for him, because the part of the castle in which his father was kept was guarded by a large dragon. Strong-arm, nothing daunted, soon found the monster, who was fast asleep, so he made short work of him by sending his sword right through his heart; at which he jumped up, uttering a loud scream, and made as if he would spring forward and seize Strong-arm; but the good sword had done its work, and the monster fell heavily on the ground, dead.

Now the Giant, who had been drinking much wine, was fast asleep in a remote part of the castle. Strong-arm had no sooner finished the Dragon, than up started the funny little boy who had opened the door. He led Strong-arm round to another part of the court-yard, where he saw his poor father, who at once sprung to his feet, and embraced him. Then Strong-arm called up his brothers, and when they had embraced their father, they soon broke his chain and set him free.

We must now return to the Little Old Woman. After her sons had started she gave way to the most bitter grief. While she was in this state, an old witch came up to her, and said she would help her, as she hated the Giant, and wished to kill him. The Old Witch then took the little Old Lady on her broom, and they sailed off through the air, straight to the Giant's castle.

Now this old Witch had great power, and at once afflicted the Giant with corns and tender feet. When he awoke from his sleep he was in such pain that he could bear it no longer, so he thought he would go in search of his missing shoe, which, like the other one he had in his castle, was easy and large for his foot. When he came to the spot where the Old Lady and her children lived, he saw his old shoe, and with a laugh that shook the trees, he thrust his foot into it, breaking through the roof that Strong-arm and Peter had put to it. The children, in great alarm, rushed about inside the shoe, and frightened and trembling, scrambled through the door and the slits which the Giant had formerly made for his corns. By this time the witch and the Little Old Lady, as also Strong-arm, his eleven brother and his father, were come up to the spot. Strong-arm and his brothers shot their arrows at him till at last he fell wounded, when Strong-arm went up to him and cut off his head. Then the father and the Little Old Woman and all their children built a new house, and lived happily ever afterwards.

Puss in Boots
Charles Perrault

There was a miller, who left no more estate to the three sons he had, than his Mill, his Ass, and his Cat. The partition was soon made. Neither the scrivener nor attorney were sent for. They would soon have eaten up all the poor patrimony. The eldest had the Mill, the second the Ass, and the youngest nothing but the Cat.

The poor young fellow was quite comfortless at having so poor a lot.

"My brothers," said he, "may get their living handsomely enough, by joining their stocks together; but for my part, when I have eaten up my Cat, and made me a muff of his skin, I must die with hunger."

The Cat, who heard all this, but made as if he did not, said to him with a grave and serious air:

"Do not thus afflict yourself, my good master; you have only to give me a bag, and get a pair of boots made for me, that I may scamper thro' the dirt and the brambles, and you shall see that you have not so bad a portion of me as you imagine."

Though' the Cat's master did not build very much upon what he said, he had however often seen him play a great many cunning tricks to catch rats and mice; as when he used to hang by the heels, or hide himself in the meal, and makeas if he were dead; so that he did not altogether despair of his affording him some help in his miserable condition.

When the Cat had what he asked for, he booted himself very gallantly; and putting his bag about his neck, he held the strings of it in his two fore paws, and went into a warren where was great abundance of rabbits. He put bran and sow-thistle into his bag, and stretching himself out at length, as if he had been dead, he waited for some young rabbit, not yet acquainted with the deceits of the world, to come and rummage his bag for what he had put into it.

Scarce was he lain down, but he had what he wanted; a rash and foolish young rabbit jumped into his bag, and Monsieur Puss, immediately drawing close the strings, took and killed him without pity. Proud of his prey, he went with it to the palace, and asked to speak with his Majesty. He was shewed upstairs into the King's apartment, and, making a low reverence, said to him:

"I have brought you, sir, a rabbit of the warren which my noble lord the Marquis of Carabas" (for that was the title which Puss was pleased to give his master) "has commanded me to present to your Majesty from him."

"Tell thy master," said the King, "that I thank him, and that he does me a great deal of pleasure."

Another time he went and hid himself among some standing corn, holding still his bag open; and when a brace of partridges ran into it, he drew the strings, and so caught them both. He went and made a present of these to the[71]

King, as he had done before of the rabbit which he took in the warren. The King in like manner received the partridges with great pleasure, and ordered him some money to drink.

The Cat continued for two or three months, thus to carry his Majesty, from time to time, game of his master's taking. One day in particular, when he knew for certain that the King was to take the air, along the river side, with his daughter, the most beautiful Princess in the world, he said to his master:

"If you will follow my advice, your fortune is made; you have nothing else to do, but go and wash yourself in the river, in that part I shall shew you, and leave the rest to me."

The Marquis of Carabas did what the Cat advised him to, without knowing why or wherefore.

While he was washing, the King passed by, and the Cat began to cry out, as loud as he could:

"Help, help, my lord Marquis of Carabas is drowning."

At this noise the King put his head out of his coach-window, and finding it was the Cat who had so often brought him such good game, he commanded his guards to run immediately to the assistance of his lordship the Marquis of Carabas.

While they were drawing the poor Marquis out of the river, the Cat came up to the coach, and told the King that while his master was washing, there came by some rogues, who went off with his clothes, though' he had cried out "Thieves, thieves," several times, as loud as he could. This cunning[72] Cat had hidden them under a great stone. The King immediately commanded the officers of his wardrobe to run and fetch one of his best suits for the lord Marquis of Carabas.

The King received him with great kindness, and as the fine clothes he had given him extremely set off his good mien (for he was well made, and very handsome in his person), the King's daughter took a secret inclination to him, and the Marquis of Carabas had no sooner cast two or three respectful and somewhat tender glances, but she fell in love with him to distraction. The King would needs have him come into his coach, and take part of the airing. The Cat, quite overjoyed to see his project begin to succeed, marched on before, and meeting with some countrymen, who were mowing a meadow, he said to them:

"Good people, you who are mowing, if you do not tell the King, that the meadow you mow belongs to my lord Marquis of Carabas, you shall be chopped as small as mince-meat."

The King did not fail asking of the mowers, to whom the meadow they were mowing belonged.

"To my lord Marquis of Carabas," answered they all together; for the Cat's threats had made them terribly afraid.

"Truly a fine estate," said the King to the Marquis of Carabas.

"You see, sir," said the Marquis, "this is a meadow which never fails to yield a plentiful harvest every year."[73]

The Master Cat, who still went on before, met with some reapers, and said to them:

"Good people, you who are reaping, if you do not tell the King that all this corn belongs to the Marquis of Carabas, you shall be chopped as small as mince-meat."

The King, who passed by a moment after, would needs know to whom all that corn, which he then saw, did belong.

"To my lord Marquis of Carabas," replied the reapers; and the King again congratulated the Marquis.

The Master Cat, who went always before, said the

same words to all he met; and the King was astonished at the vast estates of my lord Marquis of Carabas.

Monsieur Puss came at last to a stately castle, the master of which was an Ogre, the richest had ever been known; for all the lands which the King had then gone over belonged to this castle. The Cat, who had taken care to inform himself who this Ogre was, and what he could do, asked to speak with him, saying, he could not pass so near his castle, without having the honor of paying his respects to him.

The Ogre received him as civilly as an Ogre could do, and made him sit down.

"I have been assured," said the Cat, "that you have the gift of being able to change yourself into all sorts of creatures you have a mind to; you can, for example, transform yourself into a lion, or elephant, and the like."

"This is true," answered the Ogre very briskly, "and to convince you, you shall see me now become a lion."

Puss was so sadly terrified at the sight of a lion so near him, that he immediately got into the gutter, not without abundance of trouble and danger, because of his boots, which were ill-suited for walking upon the tiles. A little while after, when Puss saw that the Ogre had resumed his natural form, he came down, and owned he had been very much frightened.

"I have been moreover informed," said the Cat, "but I know not how to believe it, that you have also the power to take on you the shape of the smallest animals; for example, to change yourself into a rat or a mouse; but I must own to you, I take this to be impossible."

"Impossible?" cried the Ogre, "you shall see that presently," and at the same time changed into a mouse, and began to run about the floor.

Puss no sooner perceived this, but he fell upon him, and ate him up.

Meanwhile the King, who saw, as he passed, this fine castle of the Ogre's, had a mind to go into it. Puss, who heard the noise of his Majesty's coach running over the drawbridge, ran out and said to the King:

"Your Majesty is welcome to this castle of my lord Marquis of Carabas."

"What! my lord Marquis?" cried the King, "and does this castle also belong to you? There can be nothing finer than this court, and all the stately buildings which surround it; let us go into it, if you please."

The Marquis gave his hand to the Princess, and followed the King, who went up first. They passed into a spacious hall, where they found a magnificent collation which the Ogre had prepared for his friends, who were that very day to visit him, but dared not to enter knowing the King was there. His Majesty was perfectly charmed with the good qualities of my lord Marquis of Carabas, as was his daughter who was fallen violently in love with him; and seeing the vast estate he possessed, said to him, after having drank five or six glasses:

"It will be owing to yourself only, my lord Marquis, if you are not my son-in-law."

The Marquis making several low bows, accepted the honor which his Majesty conferred upon him, and forthwith, that very same day, married the Princess.

Puss became a great lord, and never ran after mice anymore, but only for his diversion.

East of the Sun and West of the Moon

Peter Christen Asbjornsen

East of the Sun and West of the Moon, Once on a time there was a poor husbandman who had so many children that he hadn't much of either food or clothing to give them. Pretty children they all were, but the prettiest was the youngest daughter, who was so lovely there was no end to her loveliness.

So one day, 'twas on a Thursday evening late at the fall of the year, the weather was so wild and rough outside, and it was so cruelly dark, and rain fell and wind blew, till the walls of the cottage shook again. There they all sat round the fire, busy with this thing and that. But just then, all at once something gave three taps on the window-pane. Then the father went out to see what was the matter; and, when he got out of doors, what should he see but a great big White Bear.

"Good-evening to you!" said the White Bear.

"The same to you!" said the man.

"Will you give me your youngest daughter? If you will, I'll make you as rich as you are now poor," said the Bear.

Well, the man would not be at all sorry to be so rich; but still he thought he must have a bit of a talk with his daughter first; so he went in and told them how there was a great White Bear waiting outside, who had given his word to make them so rich if he could only have the youngest daughter.

The lassie said "No!" outright. Nothing could get her to say anything else; so the man went out and settled it with the White Bear that he should come again the next Thursday evening and get an answer. Meantime he talked his daughter over, and kept on telling her of all the riches they would get, and how well off she would be herself; and so at last she thought better of it, and washed and mended her rags, made herself as smart as she could, and was ready to start. I can't say her packing gave her much trouble.

Next Thursday evening came the White Bear to fetch her, and she got upon his back with her bundle, and off they went. So, when they had gone a bit of the way, the White Bear said:

"Are you afraid?"

"No," she wasn't.

"Well! mind and hold tight by my shaggy coat, and then there's nothing to fear," said the Bear.

So she rode a long, long way, till they came to a great steep hill. There, on the face of it, the White Bear gave a knock, and a door opened, and they came into a castle where there were many rooms all lit up; rooms gleaming with silver and gold; and there, too, was a table ready laid, and it was all as grand as grand could be. Then the White Bear gave her a silver bell; and when she wanted anything, she was only to ring it, and she would get it at once.

Well, after she had eaten and drunk, and evening wore on, she got sleepy after her journey, and thought she would like to go to bed, so she rang the bell; and she had scarce taken hold of it before she came into a chamber where there was a bed made, as fair and white as anyone would wish to sleep in, with silken pillows and curtains and gold fringe. All that was in the room was gold or silver; but when she had gone to bed and put out the light, a man came and laid himself alongside her. That was the White Bear, who threw off his beast shape at night; but she never saw him, for he always came after she had put out the light, and before the day dawned he was up and off again. So things went on happily for a while, but at last she began to get silent and sorrowful; for there she went about all day alone, and she longed to go home to see her father and mother and brothers and sisters. So one day, when the White Bear asked what it was that she lacked, she said it was so dull and lonely there, and how she longed to go home to see her father and mother and brothers and sisters, and that was why she was so sad and sorrowful, because she couldn't get to them.

"Well, well!" said the Bear, "perhaps there's a cure for all this; but you must promise me one thing, not to talk alone with your mother, but only when the rest are by to hear; for she'll take you by the hand and try to lead you into a room alone to talk; but you must mind and not do that, else you'll bring bad luck on both of us."

So one Sunday the White Bear came and said, now they could set off to see her father and mother. Well, off they started, she is sitting on his back; and they went far and long. At last they came to a grand house, and there her brothers and sisters were running about out of doors at play, and everything was so pretty, 'twas a joy to see.

"This is where your father and mother live now," said the White Bear; "but don't forget what I told you, else you'll make us both unlucky."

"No! bless her, she'd not forget;" —and when she had reached the house, the White Bear turned right about and left her.

Then, when she went in to see her father and mother, there was such joy, there was no end to it. None of them thought they could thank her enough for all she had done for them. Now, they had everything they wished, as good as good could be, and they all wanted to know how she got on where she lived.

Well, she said, it was very good to live where she did; she had all she wished. What she said beside I don't know, but I don't think any of them had the right end of the stick, or that they got much out of her. But so, in the afternoon, after they had done dinner, all happened as the White Bear had said. Her mother wanted to talk with her alone in her bedroom; but she minded what the White Bear had said, and wouldn't go upstairs.

"Oh! what we have to talk about will keep!" she said, and put her mother off. But, somehow or other, her mother got around her at last, and she had to tell her the whole story. So she said, how every night when she had gone to bed a man came and lay down beside her as soon as she had put out the light; and how she never saw him, because he was always up and away before the morning dawned; and how she went about woeful and sorrowing, for she thought she should so like to see him; and how all day long she walked about there alone; and how dull and dreary and lonesome it was.

"My!" said her mother; "it may well be a Troll you slept with! But now I'll teach you a lesson how to set eyes on him. I'll give you a bit of candle, which you can carry home in your bosom; just light that while he is asleep, but take care not to drop the tallow on him."

Yes! she took the candle and hid it in her bosom, and as night drew on, the White Bear came and fetched her away.

But when they had gone a bit of the way, the White Bear asked if all hadn't happened as he had said.

"Well, she couldn't say it hadn't."

"Now, mind," said he, "if you have listened to your mother's advice, you have brought bad luck on us both, and then, all that has passed between us will be as nothing."

"No," she said, "she hadn't listened to her mother's advice."

So when she reached home, and had gone to bed, it was the old story over again. There came a man and lay down beside her; but at dead of night, when she heard he slept, she got up and struck a light, lit the candle, and let the light shine on him, and so she saw that he was the loveliest Prince one ever set eyes on, and she fell so deep in love with him on the spot, that she thought she couldn't live if she didn't give him a kiss there and then. And so she did; but as she kissed him, she dropped three hot drops of tallow on his shirt, and he woke up.

"What have you done?" he cried; "now you have made us both unlucky, for had you held out only this one year, I had been freed. For I have a step-mother who has bewitched me, so that I am a White Bear by day, and a Man by night. But now all ties are snapped between us; now I must set off from you to her. She lives in a Castle which stands East of the Sun and West of the Moon, and there, too, is a Princess, with a nose three ells long, and she's the wife I must have now."

She wept and took it ill, but there was no help for it; go he must.

Then she asked if she mightn't go with him.

No, she mightn't.

"Tell me the way, then," she said, "and I'll search you out; that surely I may get leave to do."

"Yes," she might do that, he said; "but there was no way to that place. It lay East of the Sun and West of the Moon, and thither she'd never find her way."

So next morning, when she woke up, both Prince and castle were gone, and then she lay on a little green patch, in the midst of the gloomy thick wood, and by her side lay the same bundle of rags she had brought with her from her old home.

So when she had rubbed the sleep out of her eyes, and wept till she was tired, she set out on her way, and walked many, many days, till she came to a lofty crag. Under it sat an old hag, and played with a gold apple which she tossed about. Here the lassie asked if she knew the way to the Prince, who lived with his step-mother in the Castle, that lay East of the Sun and West of the Moon, and who was to marry the Princess with a nose three ells long.

"How did you come to know about him?" asked the old hag; "but maybe you are the lassie who ought to have had him?"

Yes, she was.

"So, so; it's you, is it?" said the old hag. "Well, all I know about him is, that he lives in the castle that lies East of the Sun and West of the Moon, and thither you'll come, late or never; but still you may have the loan of my horse, and on him you can ride to my next neighbor. Maybe she'll be able to tell you; and when you get there, just give the horse a switch under the left ear, and beg him to be off home; and, stay, this gold apple you may take with you."

So she got upon the horse, and rode a long, long time, till she came to another crag, under which sat another old hag, with a gold carding-comb. Here the lassie asked if she knew the way to the castle that lay East of the Sun and West of the Moon, and she answered, like the first old hag, that she knew nothing about it, except it was east of the sun and west of the moon.

"And thither you'll come, late or never, but you shall have the loan of my horse to my next neighbor; maybe she'll tell you all about it; and when you get there, just switch the horse under the left ear, and beg him to be off home."

And this old hag gave her the golden carding-comb; it might be she'd find some use for it, she said. So the lassie got up on the horse, and rode a far, far way, and a weary time; and so at last she came to another great crag, under which sat another old hag, spinning with a golden spinning-wheel. Her, too, she asked if she knew the way to the Prince, and where the castle was that lay East of the Sun and West of the Moon. So it was the same thing over again.

"Maybe it's you who ought to have had the Prince?" said the old hag.

Yes, it was.

But she, too, didn't know the way a bit better than the other two. "East of the sun and west of the moon it was," she knew—that was all.

"And thither you'll come, late or never; but I'll lend you my horse, and then I think you'd best ride to the East Wind and ask him; maybe he knows those parts, and can blow you thither. But when you get to him, you need only give the horse a switch under the left ear, and he'll trot home of himself."

And so, too, she gave her the gold spinning-wheel. "Maybe you'll find a use for it," said the old hag.

Then on she rode many many days, a weary time, before she got to the East Wind's house, but at last she did reach it, and then she asked the East Wind if he could tell her the way to the Prince who dwelt east of the sun and west of the moon. Yes, the East Wind had often heard tell of it, the Prince and the castle, but he couldn't tell the way, for he had never blown so far.

"But, if you will, I'll go with you to my brother the West Wind, maybe he knows, for he's much stronger. So, if you will just get on my back, I'll carry you thither."

Yes, she got on his back, and I should just think they went briskly along.

So when they got there, they went into the West Wind's house, and the East Wind said the lassie he had brought was the one who ought to have had the Prince who lived in the castle East of the Sun and West of the Moon; and so she had set out to seek him, and how he had come with her, and would be glad to know if the West Wind knew how to get to the castle.

"Nay," said the West Wind, "so far I've never blown; but if you will, I'll go with you to our brother the South Wind, for he's much stronger than either of us, and he has flapped his wings far and wide. Maybe he'll tell you. You can get on my back, and I'll carry you to him."

Yes! she got on his back, and so they travelled to the South Wind, and weren't so very long on the way, I should think.

When they got there, the West Wind asked him if he could tell her the way to the castle that lay East of the Sun and West of the Moon, for it was she who ought to have had the Prince who lived there.

"You don't say so! That's she, is it?" said the South Wind.

"Well, I have blustered about in most places in my time, but so far have I never blown; but if you will, I'll take you to my brother the North Wind; he is the oldest and strongest of the whole lot of us, and if he don't know where it is, you'll never find anyone in the world to tell you. You can get on my back, and I'll carry you thither."

Yes! she got on his back, and away he went from his house at a fine rate. And this time, too, she wasn't long on her way.

So when they got to the North Wind's house, he was so wild and cross, cold puffs came from him a long way off.

"Blast you both, what do you want?" he roared out to them ever so far off, so that it struck them with an icy shiver.

"Well," said the South Wind, "you needn't be so foul-mouthed, for here I am, your brother, the South Wind, and here is the lassie who ought to have had the Prince who dwells in the castle that lies East of the Sun and West of the Moon, and now she wants to ask you if you ever were there, and can tell her the way, for she would be so glad to find him again."

"Yes, I know well enough where it is," said the North Wind; "once in my life I blew an aspen-leaf thither, but, I was so tired I couldn't blow a puff for ever so many days, after. But if you really wish to go thither, and aren't afraid to come along with me, I'll take you on my back and see if I can blow you thither."

Yes! with all her heart; she must and would get thither if it were possible in any way; and as for fear, however madly he went, she wouldn't be at all afraid.

"Very well, then," said the North Wind, "but you must sleep here to-night, for we must have the whole day before us, if we're to get thither at all."

Early next morning the North Wind woke her, and

puffed himself up, and blew himself out, and made himself so stout and big, 'twas gruesome to look at him; and so off they went high up through the air, as if they would never stop till they got to the world's end.

Down here below there was such a storm; it threw down long tracts of wood and many houses, and when it swept over the great sea, ships foundered by hundreds.

So they tore on and on—no one can believe how far they went—and all the while they still went over the sea, and the North Wind got more and more weary, and so out of breath he could scarce bring out a puff, and his wings drooped and drooped, till at last he sunk so low that the crests of the waves dashed over his heels. "Are you afraid?" said the North Wind.

"No!" she wasn't.

But they weren't very far from land; and the North Wind had still so much strength left in him that he managed to throw her up on the shore under the windows of the castle which lay East of the Sun and West of the Moon; but then he was so weak and worn out, he had to stay there and rest many days before he could get home again.

Next morning the lassie sat down under the castle window, and began to play with the gold apple; and the first person she saw was the Long-nose who was to have the Prince.

"What do you want for your gold apple, you lassie?" said the Long-nose, and threw up the window.

"It's not for sale, for gold or money," said the lassie.

"If it's not for sale for gold or money, what is it that you will sell it for? You may name your own price," said the Princess.

"Well! if I may get to the Prince, who lives here, and

be with him to-night, you shall have it," said the lassie whom the North Wind had brought.

Yes! she might; that could be done. So the Princess got the gold apple; but when the lassie came up to the Prince's bed-room at night he was fast asleep; she called him and shook him, and between whiles she wept sore; but all she could do she couldn't wake him up. Next morning, as soon as day broke, came the Princess with the long nose, and drove her out again.

So in the daytime she sat down under the castle windows and began to card with her carding-comb, and the same thing happened. The Princess asked what she wanted for it; and she said it wasn't for sale for gold or money, but if she might get leave to go up to the Prince and be with him that night, the Princess should have it. But when she went up she found him fast asleep again, and all she called, and all she shook, and wept, and prayed, she couldn't get life into him; and as soon as the first gray peep of day came, then came the Princess with the long nose, and chased her out again.

So, in the daytime, the lassie sat down outside under the castle window, and began to spin with her golden spinning-wheel, and that, too, the Princess with the long nose wanted to have. So she threw up the window and asked what she wanted for it. The lassie said, as she had said twice before, it wasn't for sale for gold or money; but if she might go up to the Prince who was there, and be with him alone that night, she might have it.

Yes! she might do that and welcome. But now you must know there were some Christian folk who had been carried off thither, and as they sat in their room, which was next the Prince, they had heard how a woman had been in there, and wept and prayed, and called to him two nights running, and they told that to the Prince.

That evening, when the Princess came with her sleepy drink, the Prince made as if he drank, but threw it over his shoulder, for he could guess it was a sleepy drink. So, when the lassie came in, she found the Prince wide awake; and then she told him the whole story how she had come thither.

"Ah," said the Prince, "you've just come in the very nick of time, for to-morrow is to be our wedding-day; but now I won't have the Long-nose, and you are the only woman in the world who can set me free. I'll say I want to see what my wife is fit for, and beg her to wash the shirt which has the three spots of tallow on it; she'll say yes, for she doesn't know 'tis you who put them there; but that's a work only for Christian folk, and not for such a pack of Trolls, and so I'll say that I won't have any other for my bride than the woman who can wash them out, and ask you to do it."

So there was great joy and love between them all that night. But next day, when the wedding was to be, the Prince said:

"First of all, I'd like to see what my bride is fit for."

"Yes!" said the step-mother, with all her heart.

"Well," said the Prince, "I've got a fine shirt which I'd like for my wedding shirt, but somehow or other it has got three spots of tallow on it, which I must have washed out; and I have sworn never to take any other bride than the woman who's able to do that. If she can't, she's not worth having."

Well, that was no great thing they said, so they agreed, and she with the long-nose began to wash away as hard as she could, but the more she rubbed and scrubbed, the bigger the spots grew.

"Ah!" said the old hag, her mother, "you can't wash; let me try."

But she hadn't long taken the shirt in hand before it got far worse than ever, and with all her rubbing, and wringing, and scrubbing, the spots grew bigger and blacker, and the darker and uglier was the shirt.

Then all the other Trolls began to wash, but the longer it lasted, the blacker and uglier the shirt grew, till at last it was as black all over as if it had been up the chimney.

"Ah!" said the Prince, "you're none of you worth a straw; you can't wash. Why there, outside, sits a beggar lassie, I'll be bound she knows how to wash better than the whole lot of you. Come in, Lassie!" he shouted.

Well, in she came.

"Can you wash this shirt clean, lassie you?" said he.

"I don't know," she said, "but I think I can."

And almost before she had taken it and dipped it in the water, it was as white as driven snow, and whiter still.

"Yes; you are the lassie for me," said the Prince.

At that the old hag flew into such a rage, she burst on the spot, and the Princess with the long nose after her, and the whole pack of Trolls after her—at least I've never heard a word about them since.

As for the Prince and Princess, they set free all the poor Christian folk who had been carried off and shut up there; and they took with them all the silver and gold, and flitted away as far as they could from the Castle that lay East of the Sun and West of the Moon.

The Tiger, the Brahman, and the Jackal

Joseph Jacobs

O nce upon a time, a tiger was caught in a trap. He tried in vain to get out through the bars, and rolled and bit with rage and grief when he failed.

By chance a poor Brahman came by. "Let me out of this cage, oh pious one!" cried the tiger.

"Nay, my friend," replied the Brahman mildly, "you would probably eat me if I did."

"Not at all!" swore the tiger with many oaths; "on the contrary, I should be forever grateful, and serve you as a slave!"

Now when the tiger sobbed and sighed and wept and swore, the pious Brahman's heart softened, and at last he consented to open the door of the cage. Out popped the tiger, and, seizing the poor man, cried, "What a fool you are! What is to prevent my eating you now, for after being cooped up so long I am just terribly hungry!"

In vain the Brahman pleaded for his life; the most he could gain was a promise to abide by the decision of the first three things he chose to question as to the justice of the tiger's action.

So the Brahman first asked a pipal tree what it thought of the matter, but the pipal tree replied coldly, "What have you to complain about? Don't I give shade and shelter to everyone who passes by, and don't they in return tear down my branches to feed their cattle? Don't whimper—be a man!"

Then the Brahman, sad at heart, went further afield till he saw a buffalo turning a well-wheel; but he fared no better from it, for it answered, "You are a fool to expect gratitude! Look at me! Whilst I gave milk they fed me on cotton-seed and oil-cake, but now I am dry they yoke me here, and give me refuse as fodder!"

The Brahman, still more sad, asked the road to give him its opinion.

"My dear sir," said the road, "how foolish you are to expect anything else! Here am I, useful to everybody, yet all, rich and poor, great and small, trample on me as they go past, giving me nothing but the ashes of their pipes and the husks of their grain!"

On this the Brahman turned back sorrowfully, and on the way he met a jackal, who called out, "Why, what's the matter, Mr. Brahman? You look as miserable as a fish out of water!"

The Brahman told him all that had occurred. "How very confusing!" said the jackal, when the recital[68] was ended; "would you mind telling me over again, for everything has got so mixed up?"

The Brahman told it all over again, but the jackal shook his head in a distracted sort of way, and still could not understand.

"It's very odd," said he, sadly, "but it all seems to go in at one ear and out at the other! I will go to the place where it all happened, and then perhaps I shall be able to give a judgment."

So they returned to the cage, by which the tiger was waiting for the Brahman, and sharpening his teeth and claws.

"You've been away a long time!" growled the savage beast, "but now let us begin our dinner."

"Our dinner!" thought the wretched Brahman, as his knees knocked together with fright; "what a remarkably delicate way of putting it!"

"Give me five minutes, my lord!" he pleaded, "in order that I may explain matters to the jackal here, who is somewhat slow in his wits."

The tiger consented, and the Brahman began the whole story over again, not missing a single detail, and spinning as long a yarn as possible.

"Oh, my poor brain! oh, my poor brain!" cried the jackal, wringing its paws. "Let me see! how did it all begin? You were in the cage, and the tiger came walking by——"

"Pooh!" interrupted the tiger, "what a fool you are! I was in the cage."

"Of course!" cried the jackal, pretending to tremble with fright; "yes! I was in the cage—no I wasn't—dear![69] dear! where are my wits? Let me see—the tiger was in the Brahman, and the cage came walking by——no, that's not it, either! Well, don't mind me, but begin your dinner, for I shall never understand!"

"Yes, you shall!" returned the tiger, in a rage at the jackal's stupidity; "I'll make you understand! Look here—I am the tiger——"

"Yes, my lord!"

"And that is the Brahman——"

"Yes, my lord!"

"And that is the cage——"

"Yes, my lord!"

"And I was in the cage—do you understand?"

"Yes—no—— Please, my lord——"

"Well?" cried the tiger impatiently.

"Please, my lord!—how did you get in?"

"How!—why in the usual way, of course!"

"Oh, dear me!—my head is beginning to whirl again! Please don't be angry, my lord, but what is the usual way?"

At this the tiger lost patience, and, jumping into the cage, cried, "This way! Now do you understand how it was?"

"Perfectly!" grinned the jackal, as he dexterously shut the door, "and if you will permit me to say so, I think matters will remain as they were!"

The Forest Bride
Parker Fillmore

There was once a farmer who had three sons. One day when the boys were grown to manhood he said to them:

"My sons, it is high time that you were all married. To-morrow I wish you to go out in search of brides."

"But where shall we go?" the oldest son asked.

"I have thought of that, too," the father said. "Do each of you chop down a tree and then take the direction in which the fallen tree points. I'm sure that each of you if you go far enough in that direction will find a suitable bride."

So the next day the three sons chopped down trees. The oldest son's tree fell pointing north.

"That suits me!" he said, for he knew that to the north lay a farm where a very pretty girl lived.

The tree of the second son when it fell pointed south.

"That suits me!" the second son declared thinking of a girl that he had often danced with who lived on a farm to the south.

The youngest son's tree—the youngest son's name was Veikko—when it fell pointed straight to the forest.

"Ha! Ha!" the older brothers laughed. "Veikko will have to go courting one of the Wolf girls or one of the Foxes!"

They meant by this that only animals lived in the forest and they thought they were making a good joke at Veikko's expense. But Veikko said he was perfectly willing to take his chances and go where his tree pointed.

The older brothers went gaily off and presented their suits to the two farmers whose daughters they admired. Veikko, too, started off with brave front but after he had gone some distance in the forest his courage began to ebb.

"How can I find a bride," he asked himself, "in a place where there are no human creatures at all!"

Just then he came to a little hut. He pushed open the door and went in. It was empty. To be sure there was a little mouse sitting on the table, daintily combing her whiskers, but a mouse of course doesn't count.

"There's nobody here!" Veikko said aloud.

The little mouse paused in her toilet and turning towards him said reproachfully:

"Why, Veikko, I'm here!"

"But you don't count. You're only a mouse!"

"Of course I count!" the little mouse declared. "But tell me, what were you hoping to find?"

"I was hoping to find a sweetheart."

The little mouse questioned him further and Veikko told her the whole story of his brothers and the trees.

"The two older ones are finding sweethearts easily enough," Veikko said, "but I don't see how I can off here in the forest. And it will shame me to have to go home and confess that I alone have failed."

"See here, Veikko," the little mouse said, "why don't you take me for your sweetheart?"

Veikko laughed heartily.

"But you're only a mouse! Whoever heard of a man having a mouse for a sweetheart!"

The mouse shook her little head solemnly.

"Take my word for it, Veikko, you could do much worse than have me for a sweetheart! Even if I am only a mouse I can love you and be true to you."

She was a dear dainty little mouse and as she sat looking up at Veikko with her little paws under her chin and her bright little eyes sparkling Veikko liked her more and more.

Then she sang Veikko a pretty little song and the song cheered him so much that he forgot his disappointment at not finding a human sweetheart and as he left her to go home he said:

"Very well, little mouse, I'll take you for my sweetheart!"

At that the mouse made little squeaks of delight and she told him that she'd be true to him and wait for him no matter how long he was in returning.

Well, the older brothers when they got home boasted loudly about their sweethearts.

"Mine," said the oldest, "has the rosiest reddest cheeks you ever saw!"

"And mine," the second announced, "has long yellow hair!"

Veikko said nothing.

"What's the matter, Veikko?" the older brothers asked him, laughing. "Has your sweetheart pretty pointed ears or sharp white teeth?"

You see they were still having their little joke about foxes and wolves.

"You needn't laugh," Veikko said. "I've found a

sweetheart. She's a gentle dainty little thing gowned in velvet."

"Gowned in velvet!" echoed the oldest brother with a frown.

"Just like a princess!" the second brother sneered.

"Yes," Veikko repeated, "gowned in velvet like a princess. And when she sits up and sings to me I'm perfectly happy."

"Huh!" grunted the older brothers not at all pleased that Veikko should have so grand a sweetheart.

"Well," said the old farmer after a few days, "now I should like to know what those sweethearts of yours are able to do. Have them each bake me a loaf of bread so that I can see whether they're good housewives."

"Mine will be able to bake bread—I'm sure of that!" the oldest brother declared boastfully.

"So will mine!" chorused the second brother.

Veikko was silent.

"What about the Princess?" they said with a laugh. "Do you think the Princess can bake bread?"

"I don't know," Veikko answered truthfully. "I'll have to ask her."

Of course he had no reason for supposing that the little mouse could bake bread and by the time he reached the hut in the forest he was feeling sad and discouraged.

When he pushed open the door he found the little mouse as before seated on the table daintily combing her whiskers. At sight of Veikko she danced about with delight.

"I'm so glad to see you!" she squeaked. "I knew you would come back!"

Then when she noticed that he was silent she asked him what was the matter. Veikko told her:

"My father wants each of our sweethearts to bake

him a loaf of bread. If I come home without a loaf my brothers will laugh at me."

"You won't have to go home without a loaf!" the little mouse said. "I can bake bread."

Veikko was much surprised at this.

"I never heard of a mouse that could bake bread!"

"Well, I can!" the little mouse insisted.

With that she began ringing a small silver bell, tinkle, tinkle, tinkle. Instantly there was the sound of hurrying footsteps, tiny scratchy footsteps, and hundreds of mice came running into the hut.

The little Princess mouse sitting up very straight and dignified said to them:

"Each of you go fetch me a grain of the finest wheat."

All the mice scampered quickly away and soon returned one by one, each carrying a grain of the finest wheat. After that it was no trick at all for the Princess mouse to bake a beautiful loaf of wheaten bread.

The next day the three brothers presented their father the loaves of their sweethearts' baking. The oldest one had a loaf of rye bread.

"Very good," the farmer said. "For hardworking people like us rye bread is good."

The loaf the second son had was made of barley.

"Barley bread is also good," the farmer said.

But when Veikko presented his loaf of beautiful wheaten bread, his father cried out:

"What! White bread! Ah, Veikko now must have a sweetheart of wealth!"

"Of course!" the older brothers sneered. "Didn't he tell us she was a Princess? Say, Veikko, when a Princess wants fine white flour, how does she get it?"

Veikko answered simply:

"She rings a little silver bell and when her servants come in she tells them to bring her grains of the finest wheat."

At this the older brothers nearly exploded with envy until their father had to reprove them.

"There! There!" he said. "Don't grudge the boy his good luck! Each girl has baked the loaf she knows how to make and each in her own way will probably make a good wife. But before you bring them home to me I want one further test of their skill in housewifery. Let them each send me a sample of their weaving."

The older brothers were delighted at this for they knew that their sweethearts were skillful weavers.

"We'll see how her ladyship fares this time!" they said, sure in their hearts that Veikko's sweetheart, whoever she was, would not put them to shame with her weaving.

Veikko, too, had serious doubts of the little mouse's ability at the loom.

"Whoever heard of a mouse that could weave?" he said to himself as he pushed open the door of the forest hut.

"Oh, there you are at last!" the little mouse squeaked joyfully.

She reached out her little paws in welcome and then in her excitement she began dancing about on the table.

"Are you really glad to see me, little mouse?" Veikko asked.

"Indeed I am!" the mouse declared. "Am I not your sweetheart? I've been waiting for you and waiting, just wishing that you would return! Does your father want something more this time, Veikko?"

"Yes, and it's something I'm afraid you can't give me, little mouse."

"Perhaps I can. Tell me what it is."

"It's a sample of your weaving. I don't believe you can weave. I never heard of a mouse that could weave."

"Tut! Tut!" said the mouse. "Of course I can weave! It would be a strange thing if Veikko's sweetheart couldn't weave!"

She rang the little silver bell, tinkle, tinkle, tinkle, and instantly there was the faint scratch-scratch of a hundred little feet as mice came running in from all directions and sat up on their haunches awaiting their Princess' orders.

"Go each of you," she said, "and get me a fiber of flax, the finest there is."

The mice went scurrying off and soon they began returning one by one each bringing a fiber of flax. When they had spun the flax and carded it, the little mouse wove a beautiful piece of fine linen. It was so sheer that she was able when she folded it to put it into an empty nutshell.

"Here, Veikko," she said, "here in this little box is a sample of my weaving. I hope your father will like it."

Veikko when he got home felt almost embarrassed for he was sure that his sweetheart's weaving would shame his brothers. So at first he kept the nutshell hidden in his pocket.

The sweetheart of the oldest brother had sent as a sample of her weaving a square of coarse cotton.

"Not very fine," the farmer said, "but good enough."

The second brother's sample was a square of cotton and linen mixed.

"A little better," the farmer said, nodding his head.

Then he turned to Veikko.

"And you, Veikko, has your sweetheart not given you a sample of her weaving?"

Veikko handed his father a nutshell at sight of which his brothers burst out laughing.

"Ha! Ha! Ha!" they laughed. "Veikko's sweetheart gives him a nut when he asks for a sample of her weaving."

But their laughter died as the farmer opened the nutshell and began shaking out a great web of the finest linen.

"Why, Veikko, my boy!" he cried, "however did your sweetheart get threads for so fine a web?"

Veikko answered modestly:

"She rang a little silver bell and ordered her servants to bring her in fibers of finest flax. They did so and after they had spun the flax and carded it, my sweetheart wove the web you see."

"Wonderful!" gasped the farmer. "I have never known such a weaver! The other girls will be all right for farmers' wives but Veikko's sweetheart might be a Princess! Well," concluded the farmer, "it's time that you all brought your sweethearts home. I want to see them with my own eyes. Suppose you bring them to-morrow."

"She's a good little mouse and I'm very fond of her," Veikko thought to himself as he went out to the forest, "but my brothers will certainly laugh when they find she is only a mouse! Well, I don't care if they do laugh! She's been a good little sweetheart to me and I'm not going to be ashamed of her!"

So when he got to the hut he told the little mouse at once that his father wanted to see her.

The little mouse was greatly excited.

"I must go in proper style!" she said.

She rang the little silver bell and ordered her coach and five. The coach when it came turned out to be an empty nutshell and the five prancing steeds that were drawing it were five black mice. The little mouse seated herself in the coach with a coachman mouse on the box in front of her and a footman mouse on the box behind her.

"Oh, how my brothers will laugh!" thought Veikko.

But he didn't laugh. He walked beside the coach and told the little mouse not to be frightened, that he would take good care of her. His father, he told her, was a gentle old man and would be kind to her.

When they left the forest they came to a river which was spanned by a foot bridge. Just as Veikko and the nutshell coach had reached the middle of the bridge, a man met them coming from the opposite direction.

"Mercy me!" the man exclaimed as he caught sight of the strange little coach that was rolling along beside Veikko. "What's that?"

He stooped down and looked and then with a loud laugh he put out his foot and pushed the coach, the little mouse, her servants, and her five prancing steeds—all off the bridge and into the water below.

"What have you done! What have you done!" Veikko cried. "You've drowned my poor little sweetheart!"

The man thinking Veikko was crazy hurried away.

Veikko with tears in his eyes looked down into the water.

"You poor little mouse!" he said. "How sorry I am that you are drowned! You were a faithful loving sweetheart and now that you are gone I know how much I loved you!"

As he spoke he saw a beautiful coach of gold drawn by five glossy horses go up the far bank of the river. A coachman in gold lace held the reins and a footman in pointed cap sat up stiffly behind. The most beautiful girl in the world was seated in the coach. Her skin was as red as a berry and as white as snow, her long golden hair gleamed with jewels, and she was dressed in pearly velvet. She beckoned to Veikko and when he came close she said:

"Won't you come sit beside me?"

"Me? Me?" Veikko stammered, too dazed to think.

The beautiful creature smiled.

"You were not ashamed to have me for a sweetheart when I was a mouse," she said, "and surely now that I am a Princess again you won't desert me!"

"A mouse!" Veikko gasped. "Were you the little mouse?"

The Princess nodded.

"Yes, I was the little mouse under an evil enchantment which could never have been broken if you had not taken me for a sweetheart and if another human being had not drowned me. Now the enchantment is broken forever. So come, we will go to your father and after he has given us his blessing we will get married and go home to my kingdom."

And that's exactly what they did. They drove at once to the farmer's house and when Veikko's father and his brothers and his brothers' sweethearts saw the Princess' coach stopping at their gate they all came out bowing and scraping to see what such grand folk could want of them.

"Father!" Veikko cried, "don't you know me?"

The farmer stopped bowing long enough to look up.

"Why, bless my soul!" he cried, "it's our Veikko!"

"Yes, father, I'm Veikko and this is the Princess that I'm going to marry!"

"A Princess, did you say, Veikko? Mercy me, where did my boy find a Princess?"

"Out in the forest where my tree pointed."

"Well, well, well," the farmer said, "where your tree

pointed! I've always heard that was a good way to find a bride."

The older brothers shook their heads gloomily and muttered:

"Just our luck! If only our trees had pointed to the forest we, too, should have found princesses instead of plain country wenches!"

But they were wrong: it wasn't because his tree pointed to the forest that Veikko got the Princess, it was because he was so simple and good that he was kind even to a little mouse.

Well, after they had got the farmer's blessing they rode home to the Princess' kingdom and were married. And they were happy as they should have been for they were good and true to each other and they loved each other dearly.

A Clever Thief

Nancy Bell

I

A certain man, named Hari-Sarman, who lived in a little village in India, where there were no rich people and everyone had to work hard to get his daily bread, got very weary of the life he had to lead. He had a wife whose name was Vidya, and a large family; and even if he had been very industrious it would have been difficult for him to get enough food for them all. Unfortunately he was not a bit industrious, but very lazy, and so was his wife. Neither of them made any attempt to teach their boys and girls to earn their own living; and if the other poor people in the village had not helped them, they would have starved. Hari-Sarman used to send his children out in different directions to beg or steal, whilst he and Vidya stayed at home doing nothing.

One day he said to his wife: "Let us leave this stupid place, and go to some big city where we can pick up a living of some kind. I will pretend to be a wise man, able to find out secrets; and you can say that you know all about children, having had so many of your own." Vidya gladly agreed to this, and the whole party set out, carrying the few possessions they had with them. In course of time they came to a big town, and Hari-Sarman went boldly to the chief house in it, leaving his wife and children outside. He asked to see the master, and was taken into his presence. This master was a very rich merchant, owning large estates in the country; but he cannot have been very clever, for he was at once quite taken in by the story Hari-Sarman told him. He said that he would find work for him and his wife, and that the children could be sent to a farm he had, in the country, where they could be made very useful.

Overjoyed at this, Hari-Sarman hastened out to tell his wife the good news; and the two were at once received into the grand residence, in which a small room was given to them for their own, whilst the children were taken away to the farm, fall of eager delight at the change from the wretched life they had been leading.

II

Soon after the arrival of the husband and wife at the merchant's house, a very important event took place, namely, the marriage of the eldest daughter. Great were the preparations beforehand, in which Vidya took her full share, helping in the kitchen to make all manner of delicious dishes, and living in great luxury herself. For there was no stint in the wealthy home; even the humblest servants were well cared for. Vidya was happier than she had ever been before, now that she had plenty to do and plenty of good food. She became in fact quite a different creature, and began to wish she had been a better mother to her children. "When the wedding is over," she thought, "I will go and see how they are getting on." On the other hand she forgot all about her husband and scarcely ever saw him.

It was all very different with Hari-Sarman himself. He had no special duties to perform and nobody seemed to want him. If he went into the kitchen, the busy servants ordered him to get out of their way; and he was not made welcome by the owner of the house or his guests. The merchant too forgot all about him, and he felt very lonely and miserable. He had been thinking to himself how much he would enjoy all the delicious food he would get after the wedding; and now he began to grumble: "I'm starving in the midst of plenty, that's what I am. Something will have to be done to change this horrible state of things."

Whilst the preparations for the wedding were going on, Vidya never came near her husband, and he lay awake a long time thinking, "What in the world can I do to make the master send for me?" All of a sudden an idea came into his head. "I'll steal something valuable, and hide it away; and when everyone is being asked about the loss, the merchant will remember the man who can reveal secrets. Now what can I take that is sure to be missed? I know, I know!" And springing out of bed, he hastily dressed himself and crept out of the house.

III

This was what Hari-Sarman decided to do. The merchant had a great many very beautiful horses, which lived in splendid stables and were taken the greatest possible care of. Amongst them was a lovely little Arab mare, the special favourite of the bride, who often went to pet it and give it sugar. "I'll steal that mare and hide it away in the forest," said the wicked man to himself. "Then, when everyone is hunting for her, the master will remember the man who can reveal secrets and send for me. Ah! Ah! What a clever fellow I am! Ah the stablemen and grooms are feasting, I know; for I saw them myself when I tried to get hold of my wife. I can climb through a window that is always left open." It turned out that he was right. He met no one on his way to the stables, which ware quite deserted. He got in easily, opened, the door from inside, and led out the little mare, which made no resistance; she had always been so kindly treated that she was not a bit afraid. He took the beautiful creature far into the depths of the forest, tied her up there, and got safely back to his own room without being seen.

Early the next morning the merchant's daughter, attended by her maidens, went to see her dear little mare, taking with her an extra supply of sugar. What was her distress when she found the stall empty! She guessed at once that a thief had got in during the night, and hurried home to tell her father, who was very, very angry with the stablemen who had deserted their posts, and declared they should all be flogged for it. "But the first thing to do is to get the mare back," he said; and he ordered messengers to be sent in every direction, promising a big reward to anyone who brought news of the mare.

Vidya of course heard all there was to hear, and at once suspected that Hari-Sarman had had something to do with the matter. "I expect he has hidden the mare," she thought to herself, "and means to get the reward for finding it." So she asked to see the master of the house, and when leave was granted to her she said to him:

"Why do you not send for my husband, the man who can reveal secrets, because of the wonderful power that has been given him of seeing what is hidden from others? Many a time has he surprised me by what he has been able to do."

IV

On hearing what Vidya said, the merchant at once

told her to go and fetch her husband. But to her surprise Hari-Sarman refused to go back with her. "You can tell the master what you like," he said, angrily. "You all forgot me entirely yesterday; and now you want me to help you, you suddenly remember my existence. I am not going to be at your beck and call or anyone else's."

Vidya entreated him to listen to reason, but it was no good. She had to go back and tell the merchant that he would not come. Instead of being made angry by this, however, the master surprised her by saying: "Your husband is right. I have treated him badly. Go and tell him I apologize, and will reward him well, if only he will come and help me."

Back again went Vidya and this time she was more successful. But though Hari-Sarman said he would go back with her, he was very sulky and would not answer any of her questions. She could not understand him, and wished she had not left him to himself for so long. He behaved very strangely too when the master, who received him very kindly, asked him if he could tell him where the mare was. "I know," he said, "what a wise and clever man you are."

"It didn't seem much like it yesterday," grumbled Hari-Sarman. "Nobody took any notice of me then, but now you want something of me, you find out that I am wise and clever. I am just the same person, that I was yesterday."

"I know, I know," said the merchant, "and I apologize for my neglect; but when a man's daughter is going to be married, it's no wonder someone gets neglected."

V

Hari-Sarman now thought it was time to take a different tone. So he put his hand in his pocket, and brought out a map he had got ready whilst waiting to be sent for, as he had felt sure he would be. He spread it out before the merchant, and pointed to a dark spot in the midst of many lines crossing each other in a bewildering manner, which he explained were pathways through the forest. "Under a tree, where that dark spot is, you will find the mare," he said.

Overjoyed at the good news, the merchant at once sent a trusted servant to test the truth; and when the mare was brought back, nothing seemed too good for the man who had led to her recovery. At the wedding festivities Hari-Sarman was treated as an honored guest, and no longer had he any need to complain of not having food enough. His wife of course thought he would forgive her now for having neglected him. But not a bit of it: he still sulked with her, and she could never feel quite sure what the truth was about the mare.

All went well with Hari-Sarman for a long time. But presently something happened which seemed likely to get him into very great trouble. A quantity of gold and many valuable jewels disappeared in the palace of the king of the country; and when the thief could not be discovered, someone told the king the story of the stolen mare, and how a man called Hari-Sarman, living in the house of a rich merchant in the chief city, had found her when everyone else had failed.

"Fetch that man here at once," ordered the king, and very soon Hari-Sarman was brought before him. "I hear you are so wise, you can reveal all secrets," said the king. "Now tell me immediately who has stolen the gold and jewels and where they are to be found."

Poor Hari-Sarman did not know what to say or do. "Give me till to-morrow," he replied in a faltering voice; "I must have a little time to think."

"I will not give you a single hour," answered the king. For seeing the man before him was frightened, he began to suspect he was a deceiver. "If you do not at once tell me where the gold and jewels are, I will have you flogged until you find your tongue."

Hearing this, Hari-Sarman, though more terrified than ever, saw that his only chance of gaining time to make up some story was to get the king to believe in him. So he drew himself up and answered: "The wisest magicians need to employ means to find out the truth. Give me twenty-four hours, and I will name the thieves."

"You are not much of a magician if you cannot find out such a simple thing as I ask of you," said the king. And turning to the guards, he ordered them to take Hari-Sarman to prison, and shut him up there without food or drink till he came to his senses. The man was dragged away, and very soon he found himself alone in a dark and gloomy room from which he saw no hope of escape.

He was in despair and walked up and down, trying in vain to think of some way of escape. "I shall die here of starvation, unless my wife finds some means of setting me free," he said. "I wish I had treated her better instead of being so sulky with her." He tried the bars of the window, but they were very strong: he could not hope to move them. And he beat against the door, but no notice was taken of that.

VI

When it got quite dark in the prison, Hari-Sarman began to talk to himself aloud. "Oh," he said, "I wish I had bitten my tongue out before I told that lie about the mare. It is all my foolish tongue which has got me into this trouble. Tongue! Tongue!" he went on, "it is all your fault."

Now a very strange thing happened. The money and

jewels had been stolen by a man, who had been told where they were by a young servant girl in the palace whose name was Jihva, which is the Sanskrit word for tongue; and this girl was in a great fright when she heard that a revealer of secrets had been taken before the king. "He will tell of my share in the matter," she thought, "and I shall get into trouble," It so happened that the guard at the prison door was fond of her, as well as the thief who had stolen the money and jewels. So when all was quiet in the palace, Jihva slipped away to see if she could get that guard to let her see the prisoner. "If I promise to give him part of the money," she thought, "he will undertake not to betray me."

The guard was glad enough when Jihva came to talk to him, and he let her listen at the key-hole to what Hari-Sarman was saying. Just imagine her astonishment when she heard him repeating her name again and again. "Jihva! Jihva! Thou," he cried, "art the cause of this suffering. Why didst thou behave in such a foolish manner, just for the sake of the good things of this life? Never can I forgive thee, Jihva, thou wicked, wicked one!"

"Oh! oh!" cried Jihva in an agony of terror, "he knows the truth; he knows that I helped the thief." And she entreated the guard to let her into the prison that she might plead with Hari-Sarman. not to tell the king what she had done. The man hesitated at first, but in the end she persuaded him to consent by promising him a large reward.

When the key grated in the lock, Hari-Sarman stopped talking aloud, wondering whether what he had been saying had been overheard by the guard, and half hoping that his wife had got leave to come and see him. As the door opened and he saw a woman coming in by the light of a lantern held up by the guard, he cried, "Vidya my beloved!" But he soon realized that it was a stranger.

He was indeed surprised and relieved, when Jihva suddenly threw herself at his feet and, clinging to his knees, began to weep and moan "Oh, most holy man," she cried between her sobs, "who knows the very secrets of the heart, I have come to confess that it was indeed I, Jihva, your humble servant, who aided the thief to take the jewels and the gold and to hide them beneath the big pomegranate tree behind the palace."

"Rise," replied Hari-Sarman, overjoyed at hearing this. "You have told me nothing that I did not know, for no secret is hidden from me. What reward will you give me if I save you from the wrath of the king?"

"I will give you all the money I have," said Jihva; "and that is not a little."

"That also I knew," said Hari-Sarman. "For you have good wages, and many a time you have stolen money that did not belong to you. Go now and fetch it all, and have no fear that I will betray you."

VII

Without waiting a moment Jihva hurried away to fetch the money; but when she got back with it, the man on guard, who had heard everything that had passed between her and Hari-Sarman, would not let her in to the prison again till she gave him ten gold pieces. Thinking that Hari-Sarman really knew exactly how much money she had, Jihva was afraid he would be angry when he missed some of it; and again she let out the truth, which he might never have guessed. For she began at once to say, "I brought all I had, but the man at the door has taken ten pieces." This did vex Hari-Sarman very much, and he told her he would let the king know what she had done, unless she fetched the thief who had taken the money and jewels. "I cannot do that," said Jihva, "for he is very far away. He lives with his brother, Indra Datta, in the forest beyond the river, more than a day's journey from here." "I did but try you," said the clever Hari-Sarman, who now knew who the thief was; "for I can see him where he is at this moment. Now go home and wait there till I send for you."

But Jihva, who loved the thief and did not want him to be punished, refused to go until Hari-Sarman promised that he would not tell the king who the man was or where he lived. "I would rather," she said, "bear all the punishment than that he should suffer." Even Hari-Sarman was touched at this, and fearing that if he kept Jihva longer, she would be found in the prison by messengers from the king, he promised that no harm should come to her or the thief, and let her go.

Very soon after this, messengers came to take Hari-Sarman once more before the king; who received him very coldly and began at once to threaten him with a terrible punishment, if he did not say who the thief was, and where the gold and jewels were. Even now Hari-Sarman pretended to be unwilling to speak. But when he saw that the king would put up with no more delay, he said, "I will lead you to the spot where the treasure is buried, but the name of the thief, though I know it, I will never betray." The king, who did not really care much who the thief was, so long as he got back his money, lost not a moment, but ordered his attendants to get spades and follow him. Very soon Hari-Sarman brought them to the pomegranate tree. And there, sure enough, deep down in the ground, was all that had been lost.

Nothing was now too good for Hari-Sarman: the king was greatly delighted, and heaped riches and honors upon him. But some of the wise men at the court suspected that he was really a deceiver, and set about trying to find out all they could about him. They sent for the man who had been on guard at the prison, and asked him many questions. He did not dare tell the truth, for he knew he would be terribly punished if he let out that Jihva had been allowed to see his prisoner; but he hesitated so much that the wise men knew he was not speaking the truth. One of them, whom the king loved, and trusted very much, whose name was Deva-Jnanin, said to his master: "I do not like to see that man, about whom we really know nothing, treated as he is. He might easily have found out where the treasure was hidden without any special power. Will you not test him in some other way in my presence and that of your chief advisers?"

The king, who was always ready to listen to reason, agreed to this; and after a long consultation with Deva-Jnanin, he decided on a very clever puzzle with which to try Hari-Sarman. A live frog was put into a pitcher; the lid was shut down, and the man who pretended to know everything was brought into the great reception room, where all the wise men of the court were gathered together round the throne, on which sat the king in his royal robes. Deva-Jnanin had been chosen by his master to speak for him; and coming forward, he pointed to the small pitcher on the ground, and said: "Great as are the honors already bestowed on you, they shall be increased if you can say at once what is in that pitcher."

VIII

Hari-Sarman thought when he looked at the pitcher: "Alas, alas, it is all over with me now! Never can I find out what is in it. Would that I had left this town with the money I had from Jihva before it was too late!" Then he began to mutter to himself, as it was always his habit to do when he was in trouble. It so happened that, when he was a little boy, his father used to call him frog, and now his thoughts went back to the time when he was a happy innocent child, and he said aloud: "Oh, frog, what trouble has come to you! That pitcher will be the death of you!"

Even Deva-Jnanin was astonished when he heard that; and so were all the other wise men. The king was delighted to find that after all he had made no mistake; and all the people who had been allowed to come in to see the trial were greatly excited. Shouting for joy the king called Hari-Sarman to come to the foot of the throne, and told him he would never, never doubt him again. He should have yet more money, a beautiful house in the country as well as the one he already had in the town, and his children should be brought from the farm to live with him and their mother, who should have lovely dresses and ornaments to wear.

Nobody was more surprised than Hari-Sarman himself. He guessed, of course, that there was a frog in the pitcher. And when the king had ended his speech, he said: "One thing I ask in addition to all that has been given me, that I may keep the pitcher in memory of this day, when my truth has been proved once more beyond a doubt."

His request was, of course, granted; and he went off with the pitcher under his arm, full of rejoicing over his narrow escape. At the same time he was also full of fear for the future. He knew only too well that it had only been by a lucky chance that he had used the word Jihva in his first danger and Frog in the second. He was not likely to get off a third time; and he made up his mind that he would skip away some dark night soon, with all the money and jewels he could carry, and be seen no more where such strange adventures had befallen him. He did not even tell his wife what he meant to do, but pretended to have forgiven her entirely for the way she had neglected him when he was poor, and to be glad that their children were to be restored to them. Before they came from the farm their father had disappeared, and nobody ever found out what had become of him; but the king let his family keep what had been given to him, and to the end believed he really had been what he had pretended to be. Only Deva-Jnanin had his doubts; but he kept them to himself, for he thought, "Now the man is gone, it really does not matter who or what he was."

The Griffin and the Minor Canon

Frank Stockton

OVER the great door of an old, old church which stood in a quiet town of a faraway land there was carved in stone the figure of a large griffin. The old-time sculptor had done his work with great care, but the image he had made was not a pleasant one to look at. It had a large head, with enormous open mouth and savage teeth; from its back arose great wings, armed with sharp hooks and prongs; it had stout legs m front, with projecting claws, but there were no legs behind—the body running out into a long and powerful tail, finished off at the end with a barbed point. This tail was coiled up under him, the end sticking up just back of his wings.

The sculptor, or the people who had ordered this stone figure, had evidently been very much pleased with it, for little copies of it, also on stone, had been placed here and there along the sides of the church, not very far from the ground so that people could easily look at them, and ponder on their curious forms. There were a great many other sculptures on the outside of this church—saints, martyrs, grotesque heads of men, beasts, and birds, as well as those of other creatures which cannot be named, because nobody knows exactly what they were; but none were so curious and interesting as the great griffin over the door, and the little griffins on the sides of the church.

A long, long distance from the town, in the midst of dreadful wilds scarcely known to man, there dwelt the Griffin whose image had been put up over the church door. In some way or other, the old-time sculptor had seen him and afterward, to the best of his memory, had copied his figure in stone.

The Griffin had never known this, until, hundreds of years afterward, he heard from a bird, from a wild animal, or in some manner which it is not now easy to find out, that there was a likeness of him on the old church in the distant town.

Now, this Griffin had no idea how he looked. He had never seen a mirror, and the streams where he lived were so turbulent and violent that a quiet piece of water, which would reflect the image of anything looking into it, could not be found. Being, as far as could be ascertained, the very last of his race, he had never seen another griffin. Therefore it was that, when he heard of this stone image of himself, he became very anxious to know what he looked like, and at last he determined to go to the old church, and see for himself what manner of being he was.

So he started off from the dreadful wilds, and flew on and on until he came to the countries inhabited by men, where his appearance in the air created great consternation; but he alighted nowhere, keeping up a steady flight until he reached the suburbs of the town which had his image on its church. Here, late in the afternoon, he lighted in a green meadow by the side of a brook, and stretched himself on the grass to rest. His great wings were tired, for he had not made such a long flight in a century, or more.

The news of his coming spread quickly over the town, and the people, frightened nearly out of their wits by the arrival of so strange a visitor, fled into their houses, and shut themselves up. The Griffin called loudly for someone to come to him but the more he called, the more afraid the people were to show themselves. At length he saw two laborers hurrying to their homes through the fields, and in a terrible voice he commanded them to stop. Not daring to disobey, the men stood, trembling.

"What is the matter with you all?" cried the Griffin. "Is there not a man in your town who is brave enough to speak to me?"

"I think," said one of the laborers, his voice shaking so that his words could hardly be understood, "that-perhaps—the Minor Canon—would come."

"Go, call him, them" said the Griffin; "I want to see him."

The Minor Canon, who was an assistant in the old church, had just finished the afternoon services, and was coming out of a side door, with three aged women who had formed the weekday congregation. He was a young man of a kind disposition, and very anxious to do good to the people of the town. Apart from his duties in the church, where he conducted services every weekday, he visited the sick and the poor, counseled and assisted persons who were in trouble, and taught a school composed entirely of the bad children in the town with whom nobody else would have anything to do. Whenever the people wanted something difficult done for them, they always went to the Minor Canon. Thus it was that the laborer thought of the young priest when he found that someone must come and speak to the Griffin.

The Minor Canon had not heard of the strange event, which was known to the whole town except himself and the three old women and when he was informed of it, and was told that the Griffin had asked to see him, he was greatly amazed and frightened.

"Me!" he exclaimed. "He has never heard of me! What should he want with me?"

"Oh! you must go instantly!" cried the two men. "He is very angry now because he has been kept waiting so long; and nobody knows what may happen if you don't hurry to him."

The poor Minor Canon would rather have had his hand cut off than go out to meet an angry Griffin but he felt that it was his duty to go for it would be a woeful thing if injury should come to the people of the town because he was not brave enough to obey the summons of the Griffin. So, pale and frightened, he started off.

'Well," said the Griffin, as soon as the young man came near, "I am glad to see that there is someone who has the courage to come to me."

The Minor Canon did not feel very brave, but he bowed his head.

'Is this the town," said the Griffin, "where there is a church with a likeness of myself over one of the doors?"

The Minor Canon looked at the frightful creature before him and saw that it was, without doubt, exactly like the stone image on the church. "Yes," he said, "you are right."

"Well, then," said the Griffin, "will you take me to it? I wish very much to see it."

The Minor Canon instantly thought that if the Griffin entered the town without the people's knowing what he came for, some of them would probably be frightened to death, and so he sought to gain time to prepare their minds.

'It is growing dark, now," he said, very much afraid, as he spoke, that his words might enrage the Griffin, "and objects on the front of the church cannot be seen clearly. It will be better to wait until morning, if you wish to get a good view of the stone image of yourself."

"That will suit me very well," said the Griffin. "I see you are a man of good sense. I am tired, and I will take a nap here on this soft grass, while I cool my tail in the little stream that runs near me. The end of my tail gets red-hot when I am angry or excited, and it is quite warm now. So you may go; but be sure and come early tomorrow morning, and show me the way to the church."

The Minor Canon was glad enough to take his leave, and hurried into the town. In front of the church he found a great many people assembled to hear his report of his interview with the Griffin. When they found that he had not come to spread rum, but simply to see his stony likeness on the church, they showed neither relief nor gratification, but began to upbraid the Minor Canon for consenting to conduct the creature into the town.

'What could I do?" cried the young man. "If I should not bring him he would come himself, and, perhaps, end by setting fire to the town with his red-hot tail."

Still the people were not satisfied, and a great many plans were proposed to prevent the Griffin from coming into the town. Some elderly persons urged that the young men should go out and kill him; but the young men scoffed at such a ridiculous idea.

Then someone said that it would be a good thing to destroy the stone image, so that the Griffin would have no excuse for entering the town; and this plan was received with such favor that many of the people ran for hammers, chisels, and crowbars, with which to tear down and break up the stone griffin. But the Minor Canon resisted this plan with all the strength of his mind and body. He assured the people that this action would enrage the Griffin beyond measure, for it would be impossible to conceal from him that his image had been destroyed during the night. But the people were so determined to break up the stone griffin that the Minor Canon saw that there was nothing for him to do but to stay there and protect it. All night he walked up and down in front of the church door, keeping away the men who brought ladders, by which they might mount to the great stone griffin, and knock it to pieces with their hammers and crowbars. After many hours the people were obliged to give up their attempts, and went home to sleep; but the Minor Canon remained at his post till early morning, and then he hurried away to the field where he had left the Griffin.

The monster had just awakened, and rising to his forelegs and shaking himself he said that he was ready to go into the town. The Minor Canon, therefore, walked back, the Griffin flying slowly through the air, at a short distance above the head of his guide. Not a person was to be seen in the streets, and they went directly to the front of the church, where the Minor Canon pointed out the stone griffin.

The real Griffin settled down in the little square before the church and gazed earnestly at his sculptured likeness. For a long time he looked at it. First he put his head on one side, and then he put it on the other; then he shut his right eye and gazed with his left, after which he shut his left eye and gazed with his right. Then he moved a little to one side and looked at the image, then he moved the other way. After a while he said to the Minor Canon, who had been standing by all this time:

"It is, it must be, an excellent likeness! That breadth between the eyes, that expansive forehead, those massive jaws! I feel that it must resemble me. If there is any fault to find with it, it is that the neck seems a little stiff. But that is nothing. It is an admirable likeness—admirable!"

The Griffin sat looking at his image all the morning and all the afternoon. The Minor Canon had been afraid to go away and leave him, and had hoped all through the day that he would soon be satisfied with his inspection and fly away home. But by evening the poor young man was very tired, and felt that he must eat and sleep. He frankly said this to the Griffin, and asked him if he would not like something to eat. He said this because he felt obliged in politeness to do so, but as soon as he had spoken the words, he was seized with dread lest the monster should demand half a dozen babies, or some tempting repast of that kind.

"Oh, no," said the Griffin; 'I never eat between the equinoxes. At the vernal and at the autumnal equinox I take a good meal, and that lasts me for ha]f a year. I am extremely regular in my habits, and do not think it healthful to eat at odd times. But if you need food, go and get it, and I will return to the soft grass where I slept last night and take another nap."

The next day the Griffin came again to the little square before the church, and remained there until evening, steadfastly regarding the stone griffin over the door. The Minor Canon came out once or twice to look at him, and the Griffin seemed very glad to see him; but the young clergyman could not stay as he had done before, for he had many duties to perform. Nobody went to the church, but the people came to the Minor Canon's house, and anxiously asked him how long the Griffin was going to stay.

"I do not know," he answered, "but I think he will

soon be satisfied with regarding his stone likeness, and then he will go away."

But the Griffin did not go away. Morning after morning he came to the church; but after a time he did not stay there all day. He seemed to have taken a great fancy to the Minor Canon, and followed him about as he worked. He would wait for him at the side door of the church, for the Minor Canon held services every day, morning and evening, though nobody came now. "If anyone should come," he said to himself, "I must be found at my post." When the young man came out, the Griffin would accompany him in his visits to the sick and the poor, and would often look into the windows of the schoolhouse where the Minor Canon was teaching his unruly scholars. All the other schools were closed, but the parents of the Minor Canon's scholars forced them to go to school, because they were so bad they could not endure them all day at home—Griffin or no Griffin. But it must be said they generally behaved very well when that great monster sat up on his tail and looked in at the schoolroom window.

When it was found that the Griffin showed no sign of going away, all the people who were able to do so left the town. The canons and the higher officers of the church had fled away during the first day of the Griffin's visit, leaving behind only the Minor Canon and some of the men who opened the doors and swept the church. All the citizens who could afford it shut up their houses and traveled to distant parts, and only the working people and the poor were left behind. After some days these ventured to go about and attend to their business, for if they did not work they would starve. They were getting a little used to seeing the Griffin; and having been told that he did not eat between equinoxes, they did not feel so much afraid of him as before.

Day by day the Griffin became more and more attached to the Minor Canon. He kept near him a great part of the time, and often spent the night in front of the little house where the young clergyman lived alone. This strange companionship was often burdensome to the Minor Canon, but, on the other hand, he could not deny that he derived a great deal of benefit and instruction from it. The Griffin had lived for hundreds of years, and had seen much, and he told the Minor Canon many wonderful things.

"It is like reading an old book," said the young clergyman to himself; "but how many books I would have had to read before I would have found out what the Griffin has told me about the earth, the air, the water, about minerals, and metals, and growing things, and all the wonders of the world!"

Thus the summer went on, and drew toward its close. And now the people of the town began to be very much troubled again.

"It will not be long," they said, "before the autumnal equinox is here, and then that monster will want to eat. He will be dreadfully hungry, for he has taken so much exercise since his last meal. He will devour our children. Without doubt, he will eat them all. What is to be done?"

To this question no one could give an answer, but all agreed that the Griffin must not be allowed to remain until the approaching equinox. After talking over the matter a great deal, a crowd of the people went to the Minor Canon at a time when the Griffin was not with him.

'It is all your fault," they said, "that that monster is among us. You brought him here, and you ought to see that he goes away. It is only on your account that he stays here at all; for, although he visits his image every day, he is with you the greater part of the time. If you were not here, he would not stay. It is your duty to go away, and then he will follow you, and we shall be free from the dreadful danger which hangs over us."

"Go away!" cried the Minor Canon, greatly grieved at being spoken to in such a way. "Where shall I go? If I go to some other town, shall I not take this trouble there? Have I a right to do that?"

"No," said the people, "you must not go to any other town. There is no town far enough away. You must go to the dreadful wilds where the Griffin lives, and then he will follow you and stay there."

They did not say whether or not they expected the Minor Canon to stay there also, and he did not ask them anything about it. He bowed his head, and went into his house to think. The more he thought, the more clear it became to his mind that it was his duty to go away, and thus free the town from the presence of the Griffin.

That evening he packed a leather bag full of bread and meat, and early the next morning he set out or his journey to the dreadful wilds. It was a long, weary, and doleful journey, especially after he had gone beyond the habitations of men; but the Minor Canon kept on bravely, and never faltered.

The way was longer than he had expected, and his provisions soon grew so scanty that he was obliged to eat but a little every day; but he kept up his courage, and pressed on, and, after many days of toilsome travel, he reached the dreadful wilds.

When the Griffin found that the Minor Canon had left the town he seemed sorry, but showed no desire to go and look for him. After a few days had passed he became much annoyed, and asked some of the people where the Minor Canon had gone. But, although the citizens had been so anxious that the young clergyman should go to the dreadful wilds, thinking that the Griffin would immediately follow him, they were now afraid to mention the Minor Canon's destination, for the monster seemed angry already, and if he should suspect their trick he would, doubtless, become very much enraged. So everyone said he did not know, and the Griffin wandered about disconsolate. One morning he looked into the Minor Canon's schoolhouse, which was always empty now, and thought that it was a shame that everything should suffer on account of the young man's absence.

"It does not matter so much about the church," he said, "for nobody went there; but it is a pity about the school. I think I will teach it myself until he returns."

It was the hour for opening the school, and the Griffin went inside and pulled the rope which rang the school bell. Some of the children who heard the bell ran in to see what was the matter, supposing it to be a joke of one of their companions; but when they saw the Griffin they stood astonished and scared.

"Go tell the other scholars," said the monster, "that school is about to open, and that if they are not all here in ten minutes I shall come after them."

In seven minutes every scholar was in place.

Never was seen such an orderly school. Not a boy or girl moved or uttered a whisper. The Griffin climbed into the master's seat, his wide wings spread on each side of him, because he could not lean back in his chair while they stuck out behind, and his great tail coiled around, m front of the desk, the barbed end sticking up, ready to tap any boy or girl who might misbehave.

The Griffin now addressed the scholars, telling them that he intended to teach them while their master was away.

In speaking he tried to imitate, as far as possible, the mild and gentle tones of the Minor Canon; but it must be admitted that in this he was not very successful. He had paid a good deal of attention to the studies of the school, and he determined not to try to teach them anything new, but to review them in what they had been studying; so he called up the various classes, and questioned them upon their previous lessons. The children racked their brains to remember what they had learned. They were so afraid of the Griffin's displeasure that they recited as they had never recited before. One of the boys, far down in his class, answered so well that the Griffin was astonished.

'I should think you would be at the head," said he. "I am sure you have never been in the habit of reciting so well. Why is this?"

"Because I did not choose to take the trouble," said the boy, trembling in his boots. He felt obliged to speak the truth, for all the children thought that the great eyes of the Griffin could see right through them, and that he would know when they told a falsehood.

"You ought to be ashamed of yourself," said the Griffin. "Go down to the very tail of the class; and if you are not at the head m two days, I shall know the reason why."

The next afternoon this boy was Number One.

It was astonishing how much these children now learned of what they had been studying. It was as if they had been educated over again. The Griffin used no severity toward them, but there was a look about him which made them unwilling to go to bed until they were sure they knew their lessons for the next day.

The Griffin now thought that he ought to visit the sick and the poor; and he began to go about the town for this purpose. The effect upon the sick was miraculous. All, except those who were very ill indeed, jumped from their beds when they heard he was coming, and declared themselves quite well. To those who could not get up he gave herbs and roots, which none of them had ever before thought of as medicines, but which the Griffin had seen used in various parts of the world; and most of them recovered. But, for all that, they afterward said that, no matter what happened to them, they hoped that they should never again have such a doctor coming to their bedsides, feeling their pulses and looking at their tongues.

As for the poor, they seemed to have utterly disappeared. All those who had depended upon charity for their daily bread were now at work in some way or other; many of them offering to do odd jobs for their neighbors just for the sake of their meals—a thing which before had been seldom heard of in the town. The Griffin could find no one who needed his assistance.

The summer had now passed, and the autumnal equinox was rapidly approaching. The citizens were in a state of great alarm and anxiety. The Griffin showed no signs of going away, but seemed to have settled himself permanently among them. In a short time the day for his semiannual meal would arrive, and then what would happen? The monster would certainly be very hungry, and would devour all their children.

Now they greatly regretted and lamented that they had sent away the Minor Canon; he was the only one on whom they could have depended in this trouble, for he could talk freely with the Griffin, and so find out what could be done. But it would not do to be inactive. Some step must be taken immediately. A meeting of the citizens was called, and two old men were appointed to go and talk to the Griffin. They were instructed to offer to prepare a splendid dinner for him on equinox day-one which would entirely satisfy his hunger. They would offer him the fattest mutton, the most tender beef fish, and game of various sorts, and anything of the kind that he might fancy. If none of these suited, they were to mention that there was an orphan asylum in the next town.

"Anything would be better," said the citizens, "than to have our dear children devoured."

The old men went to the Griffin; but their propositions were not received with favor.

"From what I have seen of the people of this town," said the monster, "I do not think I could relish anything which was prepared by them. They appear to be all cowards and, therefore, mean and selfish. As for eating one of them, old or young, I could not think of it for a moment. In fact, there was only one creature in the whole place for whom I could have had any appetite, and that is the Minor Canon, who has gone away. He was brave, and good, and honest, and I think I should have relished him."

"Ah!" said one of the old men very politely, "in that case I wish we had not sent him to the dreadful wilds!"

"What!" cried the Griffin. "What do you mean? Explain instantly what you are talking about!"

The old man, terribly frightened at what he had said, was obliged to tell how the Minor Canon had been sent away by the people, in the hope that the Griffin might be induced to follow him.

When the monster heard this he became furiously angry. He dashed away from the old men, and, spreading his wings, flew backward and forward over the town. He was so much excited that his tail became red-hot, and glowed lace a meteor against the evening sky. When at last he settled down in the little field where he usually rested, and thrust his tail into the brook, the steam arose like a cloud, and the water of the stream ran hot through the town. The citizens were greatly frightened, and bitterly blamed the old man for telling about the Minor Canon.

"It is plain," they said, "that the Griffin intended at last to go and look for him, and we should have been saved. Now who can tell what misery you have brought upon us."

The Griffin did not remain long in the little field. As soon as his tail was cool he flew to the town hall and rang the bell. The citizens knew that they were expected to come there; and although they were afraid to go, they were still more afraid to stay away; and they crowded into the hall. The Griffin was on the platform at one end, flapping his wings and walking up and down, and the end of his tail was still so warm that it slightly scorched the boards as he dragged it after him.

When everybody who was able to come was there, the Griffin stood still and addressed the meeting.

'I have had a very low opinion of you," he said, "ever since I discovered what cowards you are, but I had no idea that you were so ungrateful, selfish, and cruel as I now find you to be. Here was your Minor Canon, who labored day and night for your good, and thought of nothing else but how he might benefit you and make you happy; and as soon as you imagine yourselves threatened with a danger— for well I know you are dreadfully afraid of me—you send him off, caring not whether he returns or perishes, hoping thereby to save yourselves. Now, I had conceived a great liking for that young man, and had intended, in a day or two, to go and look him up. But I have changed my mind about him. I shall go and find- him, but I shall send him back here to live among you, and I intend that he shall enjoy the reward of his labor and his sacrifices.

"Go, some of you, to the officers of the church, who so cowardly ran away when I first came here, and tell them never to return to this town under penalty of death. And if, when your Minor Canon comes back to you, you do not bow yourselves before him, put him in the highest place among you, and serve and honor him all his life, beware of my terrible vengeance! There were only two good things in this town: the Minor Canon and the stone image of myself over your church door. One of these you have sent away, and the other 1 shall carry away myself."

With these words he dismissed the meeting, and it was time, for the end of his tail had become so hot that there was danger of it setting fire to the building.

The next morning the Griffin came to the church, and tearing the stone image of himself from its fastenings over the great door he grasped it with his powerful forelegs and flew up into the air. Then, after hovering over the town for a moment, he gave his tail an angry shake and took up his flight to the dreadful wilds. When he reached this desolate region, he set the stone griffin upon a ledge of a rock which rose in front of the dismal cave he called his home. There the image occupied a position somewhat similar to that it had had over the church door; and the Griffin, panting with the exertion of carrying such an enormous load to so great a distance, lay down upon the ground and regarded it with much satisfaction. When he felt somewhat rested he went to look for the Minor Canon. He found the young man, weak and half starved, lying under the shadow of a rock. After picking him up and carrying him to his cave, the Griffin flew away to a distant marsh, where he procured some roots and herbs which he well knew were strengthening and beneficial to man, though he had never tasted them himself. After eating these the Minor Canon was greatly revived, and sat up and listened while the Griffin told him what had happened m the town.

"Do you know," said the monster, when he had finished, "that I have had, and still have, a great liking for you?"

"I am very glad to hear it," said the Minor Canon, with his usual politeness.

"I am not at all sure that you would be," said the Griffin, "if you thoroughly understood the state of the case; but we will not consider that now. If some things were different, other things would be otherwise. I have been so enraged by discovering the manner in which you have been treated that I have determined that you shall at last enjoy the rewards and honors to which you are entitled. Lie down and have a good sleep, and then I will take you back to the town."

As he heard these words, a look of trouble came over the young man's face.

"You need not give yourself any anxiety," said the Griffin, "about my return to the town. I shall not remain there. Now that I have that admirable likeness of myself in front of my cave, where I can sit at my leisure, and gaze upon its noble features and magnificent proportions, I have no wish to see that abode of cowardly and selfish people."

The Minor Canon, relieved from his fears, lay back, and dropped into a doze; and when he was sound asleep the Griffin took him up, and carried him back to the town. He arrived just before daybreak, and putting the young man gently on the grass in the little field where he himself used to rest, the monster, without having been seen by any of the people, flew back to his home.

When the Minor Canon made his appearance in the

morning among the citizens, the enthusiasm and cordiality with which he was received were truly wonderful. He was taken to a house which had been occupied by one of the banished high officers of the place, and everyone was anxious to do all that could be done for his health and comfort. The people crowded into the church when he held services, so that the three old women who used to be his weekday congregation could not get to the best seats, which they had always been in the habit of taking; and the parents of the bad children determined to reform them at home, in order that he might be spared the trouble of keeping up his former school. The Minor Canon was appointed to the highest office of the old church, and before he died, he became a bishop.

During the first years after his return from the dreadful wilds, the people of the town looked up to him as a man to whom they were bound to do honor and reverence; but they often, a]so, looked up to the sky to see if there were any signs of the Griffin coming back. However, in the course of time, they learned to honor and reverence their former Minor Canon without the fear of being punished if they did not do so.

But they need never have been afraid of the Griffin. The autumnal equinox day came around, and the monster ate nothing. If he could not have the Minor Canon, he did not care for anything. So, lying down, with his eyes fixed upon the great stone griffin, he gradually declined, and died. It was a good thing for some of the people of the town that they did not know this.

If you should ever visit the old town, you would still see the little griffins on the sides of the church; but the great stone griffin that was over the door is gone.

The Star Lovers
Grace James

All you that are true lovers, I beseech you pray the gods for fair weather upon the seventh night of the seventh moon.

For patience's sake and for dear love's sake, pray, and be pitiful that upon that night there may be neither rain, nor hail, nor cloud, nor thunder, nor creeping mist.

Hear the sad tale of the Star Lovers and give them your prayers.

The Weaving Maiden was the daughter of a Deity of Light. Her dwelling was upon the shore of the Milky Way, which is the Bright River of Heaven. All day long she sat at her loom and plied her shuttle, weaving the gay garments of the gods. Warp and woof, hour by hour the colored web grew till it lay fold on fold piled at her feet. Still she never ceased her labor, for she was afraid. She had heard a saying:

"Sorrow, age-long sorrow, shall come upon the Weaving Maiden when she leaves her loom."

So she labored, and the gods had garments to spare. But she herself, poor maiden, was ill-clad; she recked nothing of her attire or of the jewels that her father gave her. She went barefoot, and let her hair hang down unconfined. Ever and anon a long lock fell upon the loom, and back she flung it over her shoulder. She did not play with the children of Heaven, or take her pleasure with celestial youths and maidens. She did not love or weep. She was neither glad nor sorry. She sat weaving, weaving ... and wove her being into the many-colored web.

Now her father, the Deity of Light, grew angry. He said, "Daughter, you weave too much."

"It is my duty," she said.

"At your age to talk of duty!" said her father. "Out upon you!"

"Wherefore are you displeased with me, my father?" she said, and her fingers plied the shuttle.

"Are you a stock or a stone, or a pale flower by the wayside?"

"Nay," she said, "I am none of these."

"Then leave your loom, my child, and live; take your pleasure, be as others are."

"And wherefore should I be as others are?" she said.

"Never dare to question me. Come, will you leave your loom?"

She said, "Sorrow, age-long sorrow, shall come upon the Weaving Maiden when she leaves her loom."

"A foolish saying," cried her father, "not worthy of credence. What do we know of age-long sorrow? Are we not gods?" With that he took her shuttle from her hand gently, and covered the loom with a cloth. And he caused her to be very richly attired, and they put jewels upon her and garlanded her head with flowers of Paradise. And her father gave her for spouse the Herd Boy of Heaven, who tended his flocks upon the banks of the Bright River.

Now the Maiden was changed indeed. Her eyes were stars and her lips were ruddy. She went dancing and singing all day. Long hours she played with the children of Heaven, and she took her pleasure with the celestial youths and maidens. Lightly she went; her feet were shod with silver. Her lover, the Herd Boy, held her by the hand. She laughed so that the very gods laughed with her, and High Heaven re-echoed with sounds of mirth. She was careless; little did she think of duty or of the garments of the gods. As for her loom, she never went near it from one moon's end to another.

"I have my life to live," she said; "I'll weave it into a web no more."

And the Herd Boy, her lover, clasped her in his arms. Her face was all tears and smiles, and she hid it on his breast. So she lived her life. But her father, the Deity of Light, was angry.

"It is too much," he said. "Is the girl mad? She will become the laughing-stock of Heaven. Besides, who is to weave the new spring garments of the gods?"

Three times he warned his daughter.

Three times she laughed softly and shook her head.

"Your hand opened the door, my father," she said, "but of a surety no hand either of god or of mortal can shut it."

He said, "You shall find it otherwise to your cost." And he banished the Herd Boy for ever and ever to the farther side of the Bright River. The magpies flew together, from far and near, and they spread their wings for a frail bridge across the river, and the Herd Boy went over by the frail bridge. And immediately the magpies flew away to the ends of the earth and the Weaving Maiden could not follow. She was the saddest thing in Heaven. Long, long she stood upon the shore, and held out her arms to the Herd Boy, who tended his oxen desolate and in tears. Long, long she lay and wept upon the sand. Long, long she brooded, looking on the ground.

She arose and went to her loom. She cast aside the cloth that covered it. She took her shuttle in her hand.

"Age-long sorrow," she said, "age-long sorrow!" Presently she dropped the shuttle. "Ah," she moaned, "the pain of it," and she leaned her head against the loom.

But in a little while she said, "Yet I would not be as once I was. I did not love or weep, I was neither glad nor sorry. Now I love and I weep—I am glad, and I am sorry."

Her tears fell like rain, but she took up the shuttle and labored diligently, weaving the garments of the gods. Sometimes the web was grey with grief, sometimes it was rosy with dreams. The gods were fain to go strangely clad. The Maiden's father, the Deity of Light, for once was well pleased.

"That is my good, diligent child," he said. "Now you are quiet and happy."

"The quiet of dark despair," she said. "Happy! I am the saddest thing in Heaven."

"I am sorry," said the Deity of Light; "what shall I do?"

"Give me back my lover."

"Nay, child, that I cannot do. He is banished for ever and ever by the decree of a Deity, that cannot be broken."

"I knew it," she said.

"Yet something I can do. Listen. On the seventh day of the seventh moon, I will summon the magpies together from the ends of the earth, and they shall be a bridge over the Bright River of Heaven, so that the Weaving Maiden shall lightly cross to the waiting Herd Boy on the farther shore."

So it was. On the seventh day of the seventh moon came the magpies from far and near. And they spread their wings for a frail bridge. And the Weaving Maiden went over by the frail bridge. Her eyes were like stars, and her heart like a bird in her bosom. And the Herd Boy was there to meet her upon the farther shore.

And so it is still, oh, true lovers—upon the seventh day of the seventh moon these two keep their tryst. Only if the rain falls with thunder and cloud and hail, and the Bright River of Heaven is swollen and swift, the magpies cannot make a bridge for the Weaving Maiden. Alack, the dreary time!

Therefore, true lovers, pray the gods for fair weather.

Huckleberry

Frank Stockton

MORE than a hundred and sixty-eight years ago, there
lived a curious personage called "Old Riddler." His
real name was unknown to the people in that part of the
country where he dwelt; but this made no difference, for
the name given him was probably just as good as his own.
Indeed, I am quite sure that it was better, for it meant
something, and very few people have names that mean
anything.

He was called Old Riddler for two reasons. In the first
place, he was an elderly man; secondly, he was the greatest
fellow to ask riddles that you ever heard of. So this name
fitted him very well.

Old Riddler had some very peculiar characteristics, —
among others, he was a gnome. Living underground for the
greater part of his time, he had ample opportunities of
working out curious and artful riddles, which he used to try
on his fellow-gnomes; and if they liked them, he would go
above ground and propound his conundrums to the country
people, who sometimes guessed them, but not often.

The fact is, that those persons who wished to be on good terms with the old gnome never guessed his riddles. They knew that they would please him better by giving them up.

He took such a pleasure in telling the answers to his riddles that no truly kind-hearted person would deprive him of it by trying to solve them.

"You see," as Old Riddler used to say, when talked to on the subject, "if I take all the trouble to make up these riddles, it's no more than fair that I should be allowed to give the answers."

So the old gnome, who was not much higher than a two-year old child, though he had quite a venerable head and face, was very much encouraged by the way the people treated him, and when a person happened to be very kind and appreciative, and gave a good deal of attention to one of his conundrums, that person would be pretty sure, before long, to feel glad that he had met Old Riddler.

There were thousands of ways in which the gnomes could benefit the country-folks, especially those who had little farms or gardens. Sometimes Old Riddler, who was a person of great influence in his tribe, would take a company of gnomes under the garden of someone to whom he wished to do a favor, and they would put their little hands up through the earth and pull down all the weeds, root-foremost, so that when the owner went out in the morning, he would find his garden as clear of weeds as the bottom of a dinner-plate.

Of course, anyone who has habits of this kind must eventually become a general favorite, and this was the case with Old Riddler.

One day he made up a splendid riddle, and, after he

had told it to all the gnomes, he hurried up to propound it to some human person.

He was in such haste that he actually forgot his hat, although it was late in the fall, and he wore his cloak. He had not gone far through the fields before he met a young goose-girl, named Lois. She was a poor girl, and was barefooted; and as Old Riddler saw her in her scanty dress, standing on the cold ground, watching her geese, he thought to himself: "Now I do hope that girl has wit enough to understand my riddle, for I feel that I would like to get interested in her."

So, approaching Lois, he made a bow and politely asked her: "Can you tell me, my good little girl, why a ship full of sailors, at the bottom of the sea, is like the price of beef?"

The goose-girl began to scratch her head, through the old handkerchief she wore instead of a bonnet, and tried to think of the answer.

"Because it's 'low,'" said she, after a minute or two.

"Oh, no!" said the gnome. "That's not it. You can give it up, you know, if you can't think of the answer."

"I know!" said Lois. "Because it's sunk."

"Not at all," said Old Riddler, a little impatiently. "Now come, my good girl, you'd much better give it up. You will just hack at the answer until you make it good for nothing."

"Well, what is it?" said Lois.

"I will tell you," said the gnome. "Now, pay attention to the answer: Because it has gone down. Don't you see?" asked the old fellow, with a gracious smile.

"Yes, I see," said the goose-girl, scratching her head again; "but my answer was nearly as good as yours."

"Oh, dear me!" said Old Riddler, "that won't do. It's of no use at all to give an answer that is nearly good enough.

It must be exactly right, or it's worthless. I am afraid, young girl, that you don't care much for riddles."

"Yes I do," said the goose girl; "I make 'em."

"Make them?" exclaimed Old Riddler, in great surprise.

"Yes," replied Lois, "I'm out here all day with these geese, and I haven't anything else to do, and so I make riddles. Do you want to hear one of them?"

"Yes, I would like it very much indeed," said the gnome.

"Well, then, here's one: "If the roofs of houses were flat instead of slanting, why would the rain be like a chained dog?"

"Give it up," said Old Riddler.

"Because it couldn't run off," answered Lois.

"Very good, very good," said the gnome. "Why, that's nearly as good as some of mine. And now, my young friend, did n't you feel pleased to have me give up that riddle and let you tell me the answer, straight and true, just as you knew it ought to be?"

"Oh, yes!" said the goose-girl.

"Well, then," continued Old Riddler, "remember this: What pleases you will often please other people. And never guess another riddle."

Lois, although a rough country girl, was touched by the old man's earnestness and his gentle tones.

"I never will," said she.

"That's a very well-meaning girl," said Old Riddler to himself as he walked away, "although she hasn't much polish. I'll come sometimes and help her a little with her conundrums."

Old Riddler had a son named Huckleberry. He was a smart, bright young fellow, and resembled his father in many respects. When he went home, the old gnome told his son about Lois, and tried to impress on his mind the same lesson he had taught the young girl. Huckleberry was a very good little chap, but he was quick-witted and rather forward, and often made his father very angry by guessing his riddles; and so he needed a good deal of parental counsel.

Nearly all that night Huckleberry thought about what his father had told him. But not at all as Old Riddler intended he should.

"What a fine thing it must be," said Huckleberry to himself "to go out into the world and teach people things. I'm going to try it myself."

So, the next day, he started off on his mission. The first person he saw was a very small girl playing under a big oak-tree.

When the small girl saw the young gnome, she was frightened and drew back, standing up as close against the tree as she could get.

But up stepped Master Huckleberry, with all the airs and graces he could command.

"Can you tell me, my little miss," said he, "why an elephant with a glass globe of gold-fish tied to his tail is like a monkey with one pink eye and one of a mazarine blue?"

"No," said the small girl, "I don't know. Go away!"

"Oh," said Huckleberry, "perhaps that's too hard for you. I know some nice little ones, in words of one syllable. Why is a red man with a green hat like a good boy who has a large duck in a small pond?"

"Go away!" said the small girl. "I came here to pick flowers. I don't know riddles."

"Perhaps that one was too easy," said Huckleberry, kindly. "I have all sorts. Here is one with longer words, divided into syllables. I'll say it slowly for you: What is the dif-fer-ence be-tween a mag-nan-i-mous ship-mate and the top-most leaf-let on your grand-mo-ther's bar-ber-ry bush?"

"I haven't got any grandmother," said she.

"Oh, well!" any grandmother will do," said Huckleberry.

"I can't guess it," said the small girl, who was now beginning to lose her fear of the funny little fellow. "I never guessed any riddles. I'm not old enough."

"Very well, then," said Huckleberry, "I'll tell you what I'll do. Let's sit down here under the tree, and I'll tell you one of father's riddles, and give you the answer. His riddles are better than mine, because none of mine have any answers. I don't put answers to them, for I can never think of any good ones. I met a boy once, and told him a lot of my riddles; and he learned them and went about asking people to guess them; and when the people gave them up, he couldn't tell them the answers, because there were none, and that made everybody mad. He told one of the riddles to his grandmother,—I think it was the one about the pink-eyed monkey and the wagon-load of beans——"

"No," said the small girl; "the elephant and the gold-fish was the other part of the pink-eyed monkey one."

"Oh, it don't make any difference," said Huckleberry. "I don't join my riddles together the same way every time. Sometimes I use the gold-fish and elephant with the last part of one riddle, and sometimes with another. As there's no answer, it don't matter. I begin a good many of my best riddles with the elephant, for it makes a fine opening. But, as I was going to tell you, this boy told one of my riddles to his grandmother, and she liked it very much; but when she found out that there was no answer to it, she gave him a good box on the ear, and that boy has never liked me since. But now I'll tell you a story. That is, it's like a story, but it's really a riddle. Father made it, and everybody thinks it's one of his best. There was once a fair lady of renown who was engaged to be married to a prince. And when the wedding day came round — they were to be married in one of the prince's palaces in the mountains — she was so long getting dressed — you see she dressed in one of her father's palaces, down in the valley — that she was afraid she would be late; so as soon as her veil was pinned on, she ran down to the stables, threw a wolf-skin on the back of one of the fieriest of the chargers, and springing on him, she dashed away. She was n't used to harnessing horses, and was in such a hurry that she forgot all about the bridle, and so, as she was dashing away, she found she couldn't steer the animal, and he didn't go anywhere near the prince's palace, but galloped on, and on, and on, every minute taking her farther and farther away from where she wanted to go. She could n't turn the charger, and she could n't stop him, though she tore off pieces of her veil and tried to put them around his nose, but it was no good. So when the wedding-party had waited, and waited, and waited, the prince got angry and married another lady, and nobody knows where the fair lady of renown went to, although there are some people who say that she's a-galloping yet, and trying to get her veil around the charger's nose. Now, why was it that that fair lady of renown never married? Answer: Because she had no bridal. You can say either bri-d-a-l or bri-d-l-e, because they both sound alike, and if she had had either one of them, she would have been married. This is a pretty long riddle, but it's easier than mine, because it's all fixed up right, with the answer to it and everything. You like it better than mine, don't you?"

The small girl did not answer, and when Huckleberry looked around, he saw that she was asleep.

"Poor little thing!" said Huckleberry, softly, to himself. "I guess I gave her a little too much riddle to begin with. Her mind isn't formed enough yet. But it's pretty hard on me. I wanted to teach somebody something, and here she's gone to sleep. I wish I could find that goose-girl. If father could teach her something, I'm sure I could."

So he went walking through the fields, and pretty soon he saw Lois, standing among her geese, who were feeding on the grass.

Huckleberry skipped up to her as lively as a cricket.

"Can you tell me," said he, "why an elephant with a glass globe of gold-fish tied to his tail is like the Lord High Admiral of the British Isles?"

"Was the globe of gold-fish all the elephant owned?" asked the goose-girl, thoughtfully.

"Yes," said Huckleberry. "But I don't see what that's got to do with it."

"Then the answer is," said Lois, without noticing this last remark, "because all his property is entailed."

"Well, I de-clare!" cried Huckleberry, opening his eyes as wide as they would go, "if you didn't guess it! Why, I didn't know it had an answer."

"I wish it hadn't had an answer," said the goose-girl, suddenly stamping her foot. "I wish there had never been any answer to it in the whole world. It was only yesterday that I promised Old Riddler that I would never guess another riddle, and here I've done it! It's too bad!"

"I don't think it is," cried Huckleberry, waving his little cap around by the tassel. "It's all very well for father not to want people to guess his riddles, because they've got answers and he knows what they are. But I would never have known that any of mine had an answer if you hadn't guessed this one. If you had had a riddle like this one, wouldn't you have been glad to have someone tell you the answer?"

"Yes, I would," said Lois.

"Well, then, my good girl, remember this: If a thing gives you pleasure, it's very likely that it will give somebody else pleasure. So let somebody else have a chance, and the next time you hear a riddle that you think the owner has no answer for, guess it for him, if you can." Good-by!"

And away went Master Huckleberry, skipping and singing and snapping his fingers and twirling his cap, until he came to a wide crack in the ground, when he rolled himself up like a huckleberry dumpling, and went tumbling and bouncing down into the underground home of the gnomes.

"Get out of the way!" said he to the gnomes he passed, as he proudly strode to his father's apartments. "I'm going to make a report. For the first time in my life I've taught somebody something."

When Huckleberry left her, the goose-girl stood silently in the midst of her geese. Her brow was overcast.

"How's anybody to do two things that can't both be done?" she exclaimed at last. "I'll have nothing more to do with riddles as long as I live."

■